Her mind lurched back to that kiss on the hospital floor, and the tender, comforting feel of it.

It had been the kind of kiss that soothed away her fears, acknowledged her anxieties and offered her a place to rest and refuel her tired soul.

This was not that kind of kiss. It was raw and lusty. It sent shock waves of pleasure down her spine and into her shoes, waves so intense she didn't dare open her eyes. It sent a web of tingles across the surface of her skin, a hundred fiery darts of excitement and sensation. It was the kind of kiss where the sun could have dropped out of the sky and she wouldn't have noticed.

With one arm around her waist, he slipped the other under her legs and carried her over to the couch. He fell onto it with her on top of him. She swung her legs across his and straddled him, while he cradled her head with one hand.

She looked down at him before he pulled her forward and kissed her again, even harder. Even longer.

Books by Simona Taylor

Kimani Romance

Dear Rita
Meet Me in Paris
Intimate Exposure

SIMONA TAYLOR

lives on her native Caribbean island of Trinidad—a fertile place for dreaming up scorching, sun-drenched romance novels. She balances a career in public relations with a family of two small children and one very patient man while feeding her obsession with writing.

She has also published three works of women's literary fiction under her real name, Roslyn Carrington, but it is her passion for romance that most consumes her. When not dreaming up drool-worthy heroes, she updates her website, www.scribble-scribble.com.

Intimate
EXPOSURE

SIMONA TAYLOR

KIMANI™
ROMANCE

Dedicated to my father, Trevor Carrington, who died by accident
while I was working on this novel. I think it's significant that
a primary theme of *Intimate Exposure* is fatherhood, and the
many ways in which the relationship between fathers and their
children shape their lives. My father was prouder than anyone
when I became a writer, and that meant a lot to me.

Daddy, I miss you terribly every day.

 KIMANI PRESS™

PLEASE RECYCLE

THIS PRODUCT IS RECYCLABLE

Recycling programs
for this product may
not exist in your area.

ISBN-13: 978-0-373-86214-6

INTIMATE EXPOSURE

Copyright © 2011 by Roslyn Carrington

www.kimanipress.com

Printed in U.S.A.

Dear Reader,

Thanks for picking up *Intimate Exposure.* I hope you enjoy it—I especially hope you got a kick out of Shani and Elliot's getaway to romantic Martinique. You might know I'm West Indian—I live in sunny Trinidad, in the southern Caribbean. Like most West Indians, I like to show off my islands every chance I get, so you'll often see me squeezing in a reference whenever I get the opportunity. I'm especially happy when the plot allows my characters to travel, because then I can play hostess and show you around some of my favorite places.

Even if you can't hop on a plane and come visit for yourself, you can pass by my website, www.scribble-scribble.com. There's always a breath of fresh Caribbean air waiting there for you.

I'd love it if you dropped me a line and let me know what you think about my books. You can reach me at roslyn@scribble-scribble.com. While you're at it, feel free to friend me on Facebook, MySpace or Shelfari. I also have an author page on www.Harlequin.com and www.Amazon.com.

If you prefer good old snail mail, you can reach me at: Roslyn Carrington (or Simona Taylor, either one will reach me), P.O. Bag #528, Maloney Post Office, Maloney, Trinidad and Tobago.

Till then, as we say in Trinidad, *hold it down.*

Simona

Chapter 1

It was all Yvan's fault. Yvan the Terrible, Shani called him. The world's only half Irish, half Russian, all chauvinist soul food caterer. Yvan thought his waitresses looked better in low-cut French maid uniforms, except that instead of severe black fabric under their white lace aprons, they wore dresses made of kente cloth. He insisted it made them look "more ethnic." Which was bad enough, except that even if you let the hems down (which Shani had) the skirts were all of ten inches long.

Yvan said it would bring them more tips. He was probably right, and Lord knew Shani needed them. But the scant piece of fabric that barely covered her well-shaped butt also brought more male attention—and that was the very last thing she needed right now.

So if there was anyone to blame for her current situation, it was Yvan. Backed up against a kitchen counter, clutching a silver tray loaded with Louisiana crab cakes, trying to squeeze past the inebriated owner of the sumptuous house in which she was working tonight, all she could think was: *there's really got to be a better way to make ends meet.*

She'd been working for Yvan for almost a year, so she was used to handling octopus-armed partygoers, but putting an overfamiliar man back in his place with a swiftly delivered slap would be an express ticket to the breadline. Yvan was ruthless if he felt his staff weren't playing by his many rules. Matter of fact, if you survived more than eighteen months on his payroll, you deserved a medal.

So her best course of action was diplomacy. "I really ought to…" she began.

"Don't worry, honey. There're four more lovely ladies working the party. My guests are being well fed and watered. Don't they sound happy?"

They did, indeed. It was a quarter of twelve, and the party had been going on since seven. It had started out as a sedate business affair, with some of the city's better-known corporate raiders, city officials and politicians politely nibbling at their butterflied shrimp in Creole sauce and cocktail-size yam balls on toothpicks. But after a few hours, with expensive liquor flowing, most of these upright citizens were well on their way to being plastered. Past the man's shoulder, the crowd swayed, hands in the air, booties swinging to the hip-hop beat.

But that was no excuse. She was paid to do a job. She filled her lungs with sweet, smoky air, calmed herself and insisted, "Mr. Bookman, I have to get back to work."

"Stack."

"Excuse me?"

"Stack. My first name's Elliot, but you can call me Stack." His teeth were white against skin that was the color of warm sand, and his black eyes mirrored his seductive smile.

"I'd prefer not to—"

"Relax," he cajoled. "Yvan works you girls too hard." He held up the wineglass that had been his opening gambit in the current conversational impasse. "Come on, try it. Italian wines are very good—some of the best."

"You don't say." She tried to hide her irritation. Just who did he think she was? Some little dimwit who couldn't recognize a good wine? She'd have him know she was a grown woman, a married woman—technically—who'd had her share of good red wines. But in the interest of keeping her job, she bit back the retort and instead trotted out the standard response. "Sorry, but we aren't allowed to drink on the job."

His response was loaded with suggestion: "I'm sure there're lots of things you aren't allowed to do on the job." He waved the glass of red liquid under her nose. The bouquet of the wine rivaled the scent of stronger alcohol on his breath. "But I'm not gonna tell anyone if you don't."

His mouth was intimately close to her ear. She could see his lips move as though he was speaking in slow motion. "I like 'em dark, you know," Stack confided. "Beautiful girls, dark as berries." He moistened his lips. "Black men in my position, they go for white women, you know? Or light-skinned girls. Because they can afford it, understand?"

Shani's jaw became unhinged, but Stack went on.

"But not me, I still love you dark-skinned sisters. Sweet and round in all the right places. Know what I'm saying?"

Did this man actually think that was a *compliment*? Enough was enough, Shani decided. She got a tighter grip on her plate of crab cakes and pushed aside the glass of wine, which he was still holding up before her like bait. "Mr. Bookman, if you'll excuse me…"

Before she could make it past the kitchen door, he

grasped her wrist and spun her around. "Wait just one damn second here!"

Pop, pop, pop. Something blew in her head. A fuse, a gasket, whatever was holding her back. *Crack* went the tray of crab cakes as they impacted with Bookman's face. *Squish* went the tamarind sauce as she dumped the silver bowl down the front of his shirt. And *thunk, thunk, thunk, thunk* went the cakes as they rained down on the slate tiles.

At least, she *thought* she heard those sounds, although it was possible they were only in her irate imagination, given the volume of the music and Bookman's bellow of fury. "What the hell's wrong with you?"

The white apron constricting her breasts heaved, half a beat ahead of the thudding bass of the music. "Don't you ever—"

"You're finished, lady." Bookman reached past her and grabbed a dish towel off the marble-topped kitchen island and tried to sop up the sticky brown sauce trickling down his chest. "I'm going to tell Yvan just what I think of the way he manages his staff."

Shani was beyond caring. She could feel her hand coming up, rising on its own, drawing back and preparing to deliver the much-deserved slap that had been tingling in her palm since Bookman's first off-color remark.

His response was snake-swift. He caught her by the wrist, holding her fast in spite of the sticky sauce. Shani yelped as his short nails raked furrows into her skin. "Let me go!"

"What's that?"

"You heard me. I said let me—"

"Couldn't hear you, girl. Too busy listening for an apology."

She was supposed to apologize to *him*? She twisted,

spinning around so his arm was bent at an awkward angle, and leaned her weight into it. "Let go of my hand—"

Stack winced, but his nails cut deeper. "Don't think so."

They were entangled like a snake and a mongoose. Shani could feel the effort in her arms and back, but she wasn't letting up. If he wouldn't release her, she'd make sure he'd have a sprained wrist to remind him of his mistake. She put more pressure on, the effort showing in her gritted teeth.

Stack hissed a curse. The balance of power shifted. He was male and had all the advantages that came with it: greater height and strength, backed up by pure ill will. Instead of breaking their hold, he pushed back, and it was her turn to curse. Then she found something better to do with her mouth.

Her teeth closed over the base of his thumb, sank in and held fast. She tasted tamarind sauce and pure, blind rage. Stack bellowed, and the nails digging into her skin let up. He called her a name he shouldn't have.

She would have opened her mouth to answer if she wasn't enjoying her revenge, hanging on like a pit bull with PMS. Then something weird happened. There was another hand in her line of vision, and it wasn't her tormentor's. It closed around the expensive watch on Stack's wrist and wrenched the two of them apart.

Shani staggered back, confused. There'd been two of them in the kitchen, and now…

"What's the matter, Stack? Things so bad with you these days you have to wrassle your heifers to the ground before you can climb on?"

"What?" The crudeness of the comment was like a smack across the face. Shani reeled in disbelief toward the man who'd spat it out. He was an inch or two taller than Stack, but anger made it seem like more. His body was

taut, as if poised for a brawl, unkempt hair bristling with electricity and outrage. He ignored her shocked explosion, fixing his black eyes on Stack, who was angrily rubbing the half-moon wounds on his hand and glaring from her to the interloper and back.

"Don't see how that's any of your business."

"I walk in the kitchen and see you near-raping the hired help, that becomes my business."

Hired help? Where'd he get off…? "Look," she began.

Both men ignored her. "Fine time for you to turn up, too. The invitation said seven."

The man shrugged. "I had a few things to do."

"I also recall the invitation said formal."

The man looked down at himself as if only now noticing what he was wearing: a casual, open-necked shirt and dark, relaxed-fit jeans. His smile was dry and mocking. "Hard to straddle a Triumph in a tux."

Stack snorted. "If you had a lick of respect, you'd have come in your car, rather than on that thing."

"Where's the fun in that?"

Realizing he was losing the battle, Stack turned sourly to Shani. He held up his bitten hand meaningfully. "I wonder what Yvan will say when I let him know his waitress has been chewing on something, and it ain't the hors d'oeuvres." His handsome face glittered with malice.

That was enough to sober Shani up immediately, her pleasure at her small victory evaporating like spilled booze. Getting back at this pig was one thing, but her job was another. It wasn't as though she had only herself to maintain. There was Bee to think of. She grimaced and swallowed her pride. "Mr. Bookman, please…" But Stack was already turning away.

She was left with the handsome intruder, as alone as it was possible to be, given the proximity of the liquor-fueled crowd in the next room. His sharp black eyes were slowly going her over as if looking for injury. "You okay?"

"Great." As okay as it was possible to be with her job hanging in the balance. If Bookman ratted her out, there wasn't much she could do. It would be better if, at the very least, Yvan found her working. She smoothed her hair, dropped to her knees and began picking the ruined crab cakes up off the floor.

To her surprise, the tall, lithe man squatted next to her and began to help. "Pity," he murmured as he let a few tumble onto the tray. "These look delicious. You cook them?"

Too weary for conversation, she answered shortly, "I'm a waitress, not a cook." She couldn't help adding, "For now."

"Sorry about the job," he sympathized. "But I saw what went down. If Stack's vindictive enough to squeal on you, and I can assure you he is, I can vouch for you."

Tempting, but pride made her a fool. This member of the "hired help" didn't need a stranger's intervention. "I didn't need you rescuing me then, and I don't need it now."

His face was level with hers, and for the first time it truly registered how handsome he was, in a careless, I-get-up-looking-like-this-in-the-morning kind of way. Skin like sand, eyes dark as eternity. Long nose, full lips and pointed chin.

He was saying something. "Rescue you? What, when you had your teeth sunk into his hand like a squirrel with the mother of all walnuts?" He smiled, and in the darkness of his eyes the moon came out from behind the clouds. "I wasn't rescuing you, I was rescuing Stack!"

It figured. Men knew how to stick together. "He deserved it," she pointed out.

"I bet he did," he said, and then, as if explaining the

hazards of crossing the road to a toddler, he added, "Maybe next time you'll be more careful about who you flirt with."

You could have tossed a beanbag into her gaping mouth from across the room, and won a teddy bear. "Who I *flirt* with?"

The man went purposefully on. "He's an eyeful, I'll give you that, and a charmer. But I think you just learned how fast he can turn on you."

She shot to her feet and dumped the crab cakes into the garbage, trying to bring her indignation under control. It didn't work. When she rounded on him, he was standing right behind her. "You think *I* was flirting with *him?*"

The heat of her outrage could have singed the unruly lock of hair that tumbled over his forehead. "I assumed…"

"I don't want to know what you assumed…" She stopped. She really needed to get back to work. She bit off her tirade and cut around him, heading for the doorway.

He kept pace, apologetic. "I'm sorry. It's just that Stack has a way with the ladies…"

"What, manhandling them into submission?"

"He's very charming when he's sober. Give him five minutes, and he can turn any woman into Jell-O."

"Any woman but me," she snapped.

He gave her another long, slow look and said softly, "Looks like you're different."

"Different from what? The kind of woman who'd fall for a glass of wine and an invitation to slow dance in the kitchen? I should hope so." She squinted at him suspiciously. "You seem to know that pig well enough, by the way."

She couldn't tell whether the smile he gave her was rueful or mocking. "I should. That pig's my father."

Chapter 2

Low blow, Elliot thought as the look of horror spread across the woman's dark, pretty face. She began to babble, "Oh, I... I... I had no idea." The irritation she'd shown since he'd put his foot in his mouth with that remark about flirting dissipated.

She didn't deserve such discomfort, so he hastened to reassure her. "Don't worry. *I've* called him worse—and so have a few dozen women, I bet." To put an end to the issue, he held out his hand. "I'm Elliot Bookman Jr."

She looked at his hand as if she thought he'd palmed a joy buzzer, but she shook it anyway. Her hand was warm and smooth, the hand of a woman who took care of herself. He liked that. He had to remind himself to release it within the time limit set by good manners, rather than indulge for just a few more seconds in its warm softness.

"Shani Matthieu." She was frowning, half embarrassed, half anxious to get out of there. "Mr. Bookman—"

"Elliot," he cut across with the standard joke. "My father's Mr.—"

"I need to get back to work." She brushed away a floppy lock of dark brown hair, pushing it up and over her ear in a gesture that made her seem girlish. Those hands again…

She rushed through the doorway—and careened into a shadow that had sidled in without either of them noticing.

The man was about Elliot's height, but long-limbed and thin. He was so pale as to be almost transparent, save for the ferociously glowing freckles. His eyes were the color of brackish Florida swamp water, the kind that hid lurking gators. A black tuxedo draped over his thin frame made him look like Jack Skellington in Tim Burton's *The Nightmare Before Christmas*. The kente-cloth cummerbund looped around his waist immediately identified him as the aforementioned Yvan.

"Shani!" His voice was a Yoda-like rasp. "What's this about you biting my client? And hitting him with a tray?"

She hit Stack with a tray? Elliot regretted having missed that part. Then he noticed his father standing behind him, glowering, and decided the situation was too grim—for Shani at least—to merit a chuckle.

Shani drew in her lip, her beautifully shaped teeth working at the full, wine-tinted flesh. For a second he thought she mightn't answer, but she squared herself and said resolutely. "He was getting fresh with me."

"How fresh does a guy got to get for you to *bite him?*"

"Fresh enough. He put his hand on me and I asked him to stop.…"

"That's a lie!" Stack swayed a little, and Elliot knew it

wouldn't be long before he passed out. "The crazy chick bit me for no reason!"

"Why would I bite you for no reason?"

Another waitress arrived on the scene and hesitated before snatching up a tray of tidbits and scurrying off as if afraid Yvan's anger would spill over in her direction.

Fat chance. Yvan was totally focused on his current victim. "Little lady, jobs are hard to come by, especially with bosses as patient as me."

Elliot was surprised Shani didn't snort.

"This is your only warning. I want you to apologize to Mr. Bookman."

"What?"

Yvan confirmed his demand with an insistent nod. "You apologize, and maybe, just maybe, you'll still have a job by the end of the night."

The tortured look on Shani's face was too much for Elliot. He could practically hear the scales shifting back and forth as she tried to determine which was worth more: her job or her pride? Her lips parted, and the tip of her tongue appeared. The gesture was jarringly erotic, which was an odd response to have, given that the situation was so serious. She inhaled, looked about to speak and stopped again. Facing her, Yvan frowned like an old schoolmaster about to administer a whippin'. Behind him, Stack looked victorious.

She closed her eyes and plunged in. "Mr. Bookman..." she began.

This was wrong. Elliot stepped forward, shielding her from the ire of her employer and his father's unfounded self-righteousness. "The lady has nothing to apologize for. I saw what happened. My father was getting out of line, and she defended herself."

Shani gave a small squeak. "I told you I don't need help!"

"I know, but right is right. You don't need to apologize." He speared his father with a look. "Does she, Stack?"

Stack shifted, looking guilty. "Well, maybe I misunderstood…."

"She'll apologize because I tell her to," Yvan ground out. "Shani…" He pointed at Stack as if he was showing a naughty dog the way out.

She lifted her head like an innocent woman facing a firing squad. "I'm sorry, Mr. Bookman. Please…" She swallowed hard; Elliot could see movement at the base of her throat, and that movement drew his eyes downward to the cleavage that swelled out the top of her plunging neckline. She didn't need the push-up bra she was wearing. He dragged his eyes to her face again as she begged, "Please, forgive…" Then she stopped, and another look crossed her face. Not outrage, not embarrassment, not discomfort. Something else, and it scared him.

She slipped her hand into her pocket. Yvan saw the movement, reptilian eyes swiveling down. "Don't tell me…" he began.

What the hell?

She withdrew a small cell phone and looked at it as if it was the detonator for a nuclear weapon. It must have been on silent, because nobody had heard it ring.

"I've explicitly told you, all of you, you are not allowed to carry your phones on the job!" Yvan was in a fine lather. Something told Elliot that this was his usual state of being.

Shani gave him half a second's glance. "You know my situation, Yvan."

"I don't give a pickled monkey's butt about your situation."

"Hello?" Shani's voice was a whisper. Elliot's eyes were riveted to her face, beyond curiosity. Under the plum-dark skin, the blood drained. "I'll be right there." She clicked the phone shut. "It's Bee," she said to Yvan.

Bee? What bee? He half expected to see one buzzing around their heads.

If you'd set a spirit level along Yvan's mouth, the bubble would have been dead center. "I don't want to hear it."

"I need to go. Now."

Yvan lifted his hand and checked his watch. "Your tail is mine for another hour and forty minutes."

"Bee's sick, and I'm going to her."

"You do that, and..." He didn't finish the threat.

Shani ripped off the silly apron she was wearing and threw it down. "You want to fire me? Consider me fired. But please, Yvan, ask Ralph to give me a lift to the other side of Ventura. Maybe I could catch a late bus. There's nothing running here in Belmont tonight."

"Ralph drives a catering truck, not a taxi. Besides, we're busy tonight." He added meaningfully, "We're one hand short." The scarecrow of a man swooped down and scooped up the apron, tucking it under his arm, then stalked off.

That left three of them. The events of the last minute and a half seemed to have gotten through to Stack. Instead of basking in his petty triumph, he looked abashed, but Elliot knew his father wasn't man enough to say he was sorry unless it suited him. Stack's eyes took in Shani's stricken face and then he, too, slunk away.

And then there were two. Elliot put his hands on his hips and took in the pain on Shani's face. He'd known this woman only ten minutes, but inexplicably he was hurting for her. "You okay?"

She looked at him as though he'd asked the world's most asinine question. "No."

"What's the problem? What bee are you talking about?"

"My daughter," she answered irritably, as if he should have known. "Béatrice."

"Ah." Now he understood. "She's sick?"

Shani nodded wearily. "She had a fever when I left home this evening." She found her purse next to the broom cupboard. As she shouldered it, he noticed a thin wedding band on her finger. For some reason, that disappointed him.

"Was that your husband on the phone?"

She turned and wrenched open the kitchen door, which gave side access to his father's garage and, beyond it, the broad driveway. "That was my sitter. My baby's worse. Her fever's a hundred and four." She slipped through the doorway and into the darkened garage.

He hurried to keep up with her. "Where're you going?"

Her look made him feel as if his IQ didn't graze eighty. "I'm taking her to the hospital." She twisted, looking for the garage light, the better to see her way out. He found it easily and clicked it on.

"Let me rephrase that. How are you getting there? Yvan said—"

"I heard what Yvan said. I'm walking to the bus stop."

"But there aren't any—"

"Night buses that pass through Belmont. I know." He could see her legs flash in the floodlights, hear her heels click on the driveway. "I'm walking to Ventura."

"That's two miles away!"

She didn't even glance in his direction. Her determined mouth barely moved as she told him, "Then I better get to walking." A stiff, late-September wind stirred her hair. She didn't have a coat on, and that dress of hers, what passed for a dress, barely brushed the tops of her thighs.

Elliot watched as she hurried away, her hips rolling in her haste, legs moving swiftly past each other. Seeing a mother so concerned for her child's well-being that she was willing to trot across town on heels too high for waitressing stirred something in him. "Shani, wait!"

She half turned, frowning at him for interrupting her pace.

He ran down the path, grasping her by the arms. "Wait."

She looked down at the hands he'd placed on her, brows together, and when he read on her face the indignation at being restrained by a second Bookman in one night, he let go. The lady had already proved she didn't mind biting—and not in a good way.

"I have…to get…to my daughter," she explained carefully. "Fast."

The fear in her eyes made his heart constrict. "It's too late. Too cold."

"I don't have a choice." She resumed walking as though her pace had never been interrupted.

He wasn't explaining himself right, dammit! "Wait!" As he stopped her again, she sucked in a breath. He was sure she was about to scream, so he talked fast. "Just give me ten seconds, all right?"

"Why?"

"I'll take you."

"What?"

He left her standing there and sprinted back to the kitchen. The Triumph wasn't the best mode of transport for what he had in mind. He snagged his father's car keys without a second thought and darted back outside.

The burgundy Lexus chirped a friendly welcome as he

unlocked it. He rammed the keys into the ignition with less respect than such a machine deserved and, not even bothering to let it warm up, slammed it into gear and nosed it down to where she was waiting. As he drew alongside, her already-arched brows lifted just so much higher. He leaped out, opened the passenger door and bundled her in. She complied, more bewildered than anything else, letting him click her seat belt into place before he leaped back into his seat again and hit the gas.

She was staring at his face, still puzzled. "Why're you doing this?"

Why, indeed? "Just trying to help," he explained lamely. "I'd hate to know a child was sick and I didn't do anything about it."

"Oh." She was still examining his face, but whether she was looking for an ulterior motive or asking herself what she'd done to deserve the random kindness of a stranger, he couldn't tell. "Thank you."

Again, that strange ache inside him, for her. What kind of sad creature was this, so unaccustomed to receiving kindness that it took her by surprise when she found it? And where was her husband, anyway? Shouldn't he be doing this? "Besides," he added, joking to relieve his tension, and hers, "I need brownie points in heaven. God knows I've racked up enough for the other team."

She smiled weakly and relaxed into her seat. "Thank you," she said again. It came from somewhere deep inside her.

"So, where to?"

"Catarina."

He nodded. They were already approaching Ventura, a pleasant neighborhood that formed a buffer between the genteel suburbs and the busy city. From there it was just a minute or two to the highway on-ramp. On an ordinary day, it would take maybe forty minutes to get to the heart of Santa Amata. But it was well after midnight on a Saturday, and, after all, this was a Lexus, not a station wagon. They made it in twenty.

He looked covertly over at her. Her eyes were taking in every detail of the custom interior of the vehicle, the lovingly polished wood finishing, the muted glow of the array of dials and screens that illuminated her face. He saw her extend one finger and slowly stroke the leather on which she was sitting, and he smiled. It gave him an irrational, childish pleasure to share this little luxury with her. He had a feeling her life wasn't filled with much of that.

She spoke only to give directions, and he was grateful. Sometimes when you offered a person a ride, they felt obligated to make conversation, to fill the air with irrelevant chatter. She wasn't the type to indulge in that nonsense, and he liked her for that.

Catarina was on the other side of Santa Amata, a slightly…more lived-in side of town. A few blocks beyond Independence Avenue, the city's main artery, the streets grew narrower, the buildings just a shade shabbier. It was chilly—which reminded Elliot he didn't have his coat on, either—but many of the bars had their doors thrown open, and he could hear music spilling out. Trees were beginning to shed their leaves; the wind danced with them in the street as cars swooshed past.

"Left on Bagley," she told him, and he turned onto the street without a word. It was lined with brownstones and shop fronts. Most of the houses had small family businesses downstairs, with living quarters upstairs. The occasional building that rose past three or four floors looked out of place next to the squat two-story houses beside them.

"Here." She pointed, and he pulled smoothly to the curb

in front of one of the older buildings on the street. The bottom floor was occupied by a restaurant that was still open. A flickering sign above the door said Old Seoul in English, and, presumably, the same thing in Korean. The clinking of glasses and the sound of laughter spilled through the doors and open windows, and the scents of hot oil, fish and spicy meat reminded him that he'd turned up five hours late for dinner, more out of a desire to get on his father's nerves than anything else. He was beginning to regret that decision.

Shani took out a bunch of large, cumbersome metal keys and unlocked a gate that was barely visible at the side of the restaurant. She let herself through it without a word to him, but he followed closely, up a flight of stairs that would have been better lit, if he'd had anything to say about it. They'd barely reached the first landing when there was a shout from below.

She stopped so fast he almost stumbled into her from behind.

"Shani!" The voice was below them but coming up fast. Elliot stopped shoulder to shoulder with Shani as she leaned over the rusting banister to see a small Asian man taking the stairs two by two. He was dressed in a colorful embroidered tunic with long square sleeves, way too elaborate for someone who was just kicking it on a Saturday night, so he guessed the man worked in, or more likely owned, the restaurant downstairs. "Special Delivery letter for you!"

She looked puzzled, and for a few moments she didn't hold out her hand to take the proffered letter. She eventually did, turning it over so she could see the return address…and then the night went quiet. He knew that, logically, the music, laughter and chatter were still rising from downstairs. He knew the night owls were still hooting and cars were still rumbling past, but he couldn't hear them. Because for the second time in less than an hour, he was seeing the blood leech out from under this sad woman's dusky skin, and he didn't like it.

The middle-aged man standing two steps below squinted at her through thick glasses. "You well?"

She nodded, but just barely. "I'm fine, Mr. Pak. Thank you."

The man waited, Elliot waited, for her to tear open the envelope, to do something, but she held it in both hands and stared at it, weighed it, ran her fingers along the address label as if they were sensitive enough to feel the indentations of the printed letters, but she didn't open it.

Eventually, Mr. Pak nodded and returned downstairs. After he was long gone…it could have been seconds, it could have been minutes…Shani still hadn't made any move. Elliot watched her, not even pretending not to stare, taking full advantage of the fact that she was barely aware of his presence. Her dark skin had that mellow smoothness that came from good genes, although he could tell, too, that she groomed herself carefully. He was sure she did everything carefully.

She'd nervously licked off most of the frosty lipstick she'd been wearing, leaving her lips bare. The lower one was full, almost pouty, making him think of moist fruit. Her dark, straight hair had been neatly pinned up at the start of the evening, he guessed. Now it fell in wisps about her face. He found himself wanting to reach out, wind it up at the crown of her head and pin it back into place for her. He had to put his hands into his pockets to quell the impulse.

He brought his head close, stifling his curiosity to read the envelope that so mesmerized her, more interested in reading her eyes. But in them, he could see nothing. Gently, he called her name.

She looked up, startled to find him still there. "Huh?"

"Aren't you going to open it?"

"Open what?"

He tapped the heavy paper object in her hands. "Your letter."

She looked down at it again, contemplatively, and then shook her head. "I don't have to. It's from my attorney. I know what it says."

Why was it that letters from attorneys never bore good news? How come nobody ever got a letter from an attorney saying *congratulations, you just inherited three million dollars from an uncle you never knew you had?*

He asked with a chill of anticipation, "What's it say, then?"

Her eyes held his, and the agony in them kept him riveted. "It says I…" She tried again. "It says my divorce is final. My marriage is over."

Chapter 3

No job. Sick daughter. And now…this. Shani read and reread the names and addresses on the envelope, both hers on the front and her attorney's on the back. Inside it were the shredded, tattered, decomposing remnants of the past five years of her life. Knowing it was coming didn't soften the blow any.

And a blow it was; a sucker punch to the gut that obliterated any fancified notions she might still be holding about Christophe and the love she'd had for him. Where was he anyway? Back home in Martinique, most likely. And, if she knew him—and she did—out celebrating his freedom in a Fort-de-France bar, or in the bed of some young Martiniquaise with more libido than sense.

She felt the cold rails of the balcony under her fingers, steadying her as she swayed. Aching so deep inside she wished she could reach in and tear out the organ that was causing her so much hurt. Her wedding band, a little loose these days since she'd lost a few pounds, constricted. If the vein in the fourth finger led directly to the heart, as the ancients believed, she wouldn't need to rip her heart out. It would shrivel and die all on its own for lack of blood flow.

There was a movement next to her, a light hand on her forearm and a voice in her ear. "Shani."

Elliot. She knew he was there, but his touch and voice startled her anyway. She tried to focus on his face. "Yes?"

"Maybe you should go inside. Have a glass of water. Sit for a minute."

Her rattling thoughts aligned themselves in some semblance of order. Inside. Right. She nodded. She patted herself down for her keys before she remembered they were clutched in her hand. She tried to fit the key in the lock, but it wouldn't go. Wrong one. She tried again, the soft scratching sound of metal against metal amplified ten times.

"Let me." Elliot's cool hands pried the keys from her incompetent fingers and he slid them into the lock. Easily. As though he was used to it.

The tumblers rolled over inside the lock, but he didn't have the chance to open the door. It was snatched from his hand, startling them both. Gina Pak was standing there in the minuscule hallway, panting a little. She was even tinier than her father, glossy hair pulled back in a ponytail, wearing a red T-shirt and jeans, both of which were damp.

"Shani!" she exclaimed. "I'm sorry I didn't get the door right away. I was giving Béatrice a sponge bath. She's up to a hundred and five. And she threw up, twice."

Bee! Panic and shame. For a full five minutes, Christophe had managed to shove her poor baby from the forefront of her mind. Did he still exert such a power over her, that on a night as awful as this, she could forget she was on a rescue mission?

"Where's she?" she asked, even though she knew.

Gina pointed. Without looking at the wretched envelope again, she threw it to the floor and hastened to the bedroom, which she shared with her daughter. The room was decorated more like a child's nursery than a room in which an adult slept. It was bright yellow, her daughter's favorite color, and strewn with enough bee motifs to make Sting himself gag. A bee mobile swayed over the bed, cartoon bees smiled down from the walls and bee suncatchers dangled behind drawn curtains. Bee lived up to her name.

She was lying on her back. Her thick hair, which usually sprang up all over in a cheery mop, was damp from the bath. She had nothing on but a pair of panties and a yellow cotton Winnie the Pooh T-shirt. Her limp limbs were carelessly sprawled, her small, dark, pointed face slack. Eyes fire-bright. Bee spotted her and managed a smile. "Mama!"

Shani reached to smooth the hair from Bee's brow, but Elliot was in the way, on his knees at the child's bedside, lifting each eyelid with his thumbs and examining her eyes, then her nostrils and mouth, tilting her head to each side to look into her ears, too.

Shani was too stunned and confused to move.

"How old is she?" he asked.

"What the hell are you doing?"

"How old is she?"

Not wanting to be left out of the conversation, Bee piped up. "I'm three and a half!"

"You are? You're a really big girl!" Elliot was soft-voiced, indulgent, his hands still working on her.

Bee watched him with a mixture of curiosity and suspicion, her bleary eyes trying to focus. "You a doctor?"

"No, I'm not, but I'm just gonna check you out, if you let me." He tenderly ran his fingers along her throat then lifted her shirt and carefully looked over her torso.

"No blotches," he murmured. "That's good." Strong fingers encircled the tiny wrist, and he fixed his eyes on his watch, counting pulse beats.

A scary thought crossed Bee's mind, and she gave him a panicked look. "No shots! No shots!" She lifted her eyes to her mother, pleading for her intervention if a needle should appear.

For Shani, that was too much. Elliot looked as though he knew what he was doing; she certainly hadn't a clue what to do herself, but her territorial instincts were aroused, her hackles up. "Elliot, I asked you a question."

He turned to Gina, who was as puzzled as she was. "Has she eaten anything this evening?"

"Not much."

"Drinking okay? Thirsty?"

Bee pouted, as if she suspected that any second now, one of the grown-ups was going to try to force something into her. "No! Not thirsty!"

Elliot mumbled something and patted the damp hair. Bee relaxed a little, sinking back into the pillows, but still frowned suspiciously at the adults surrounding her.

Gina shook her head. "She didn't want her juice, or water. I made her take a few sips, but—"

That was enough. Shani shouldered Elliot aside and threw her arms around her daughter. The child's skin was on fire. He didn't resist, didn't look the least bit offended.

"You said you aren't a doctor…"

"No, but I know what I'm doing."

"How, exactly?"

He shrugged. "Peace Corps. Two years in Haiti after college."

She was momentarily stunned. A member of the wealthy Bookman clan, in the Peace Corps?

Without offering any further explanation, he extricated a blanket from the pile of rumpled bedding and seemed about to reach for Bee again, but then he thought better of it and held it out to Shani. "Wrap her up. It's cold out."

Shani did as she was told. Bee didn't resist, which was scary in itself. Usually, getting any article of clothing onto her daughter required a chase around the bed, three or four laps at least, and maybe a foray into the living room. But Bee was as boneless and unresisting as a sleeping cat. As she lifted the hot little bundle into her arms, Bee wound her hands around her neck, face pressed against her breast.

Elliot followed her to the door. He turned to Gina, who was hovering, her expression a mixture of concern for Bee and frank curiosity over Elliot's sudden appearance.

"This is Elliot," Shani informed the teenager belatedly. And to Elliot, "This is Gina, Mr. Pak's daughter. She's seventeen. Her real name's Jin, but, well, everyone calls her..." She was aware that she was babbling. She stopped herself. "She babysits for me."

Elliot nodded, gravely extending a hand. Then he was all business, opening her front door and preceding her outside. "We're going to Immaculate Heart Pediatric," he informed Gina.

"She gonna be all right?" Gina asked.

Elliot's eyes were on her, not Gina. "I think so. A high fever doesn't mean anything awful on its own. It's probably just an infection."

Oh, thank you, Jesus. She let Elliot propel her into the backseat, allowing him to buckle the seat belt over her lap before she settled her daughter in her arms. In the absence of a car seat, it'd have to do.

He sensed her apprehension. "I'll get you there safely," he promised. "Both of you."

They pulled to a screeching stop in the hospital parking lot. Elliot hopped out and looked in through the window at Shani as she struggled in the backseat with Bee's dead-weight. "How's the baby?"

"Sleeping," Shani answered. "Still hot."

"Then we'd better get in there." He jerked his chin in the direction of the entrance to the E.R.

It was next to impossible to emerge from the car holding Bee, but Elliot opened the back door and gently, as if lifting something infinitely precious, eased her daughter from her lap.

Shani got out, feeling the sting of pins and needles run through her legs as blood rushed back into them. It had gotten colder. She stamped on the ground, found her land legs again and held her arms out for her daughter. But Elliot shook his head, cradling Bee as though he'd known her since the day she was born. "Keep your strength. You'll need it." She couldn't decide whether to be grateful or outraged.

Of one accord, they moved toward the doors. "You didn't have to do this," she pointed out.

His mouth curved, and he shrugged it off.

Maybe it was nothing to him, a little lost sleep and a missed dinner, but she needed for him to know that to her, his small gesture meant everything. "My daughter..." As she walked, she searched for words. "Bee's all I have, now." She tried not to think of Christophe. *He* hadn't been hers for a long time.

His expression was so compassionate, it hurt to look

at him. "She'll be okay, I promise you. And I don't mind doing this. Really."

Which was a good thing, because at that moment Bee was jolted out of her exhausted, fever-tormented sleep. She went rigid, threw open her startled brown eyes, flung out thin, stiff limbs and threw up down the front of his shirt.

Chapter 4

Shani reacted immediately, reaching out to help tilt Bee's head so that most of the clear fluid spurted onto the ground.

"Elliot, I'm so—"

"It's all right."

She fumbled through her bag, cursing the clutter, and pulled out a packet of baby wipes. "At least let me…I'm so sorry!" She dabbed at the wet mark on his shirt, cringing at what he must be thinking. She was a mother, used to dealing with all manner of bodily fluids, but this was a single man. Baby upchuck was probably at the top of his gross-out list.

"Relax. She's done now."

She held out her arms, expecting him to hand Bee over as if she was an armload of contraband, but he was walking again. "Better get her inside."

It was a choice between standing in the cold parking lot

and following. She followed. "I'll get your shirt cleaned," she promised.

He threw her an amused, patient look over the fluffy blanket-covered bump in his arms. "The shirt'll wash." He stepped aside to let her get the door. She brushed past a security guard who was lightly dozing on his feet and heaved against the heavy glass door under a large sign that read EMERGENCY in white on red.

Elliot found them a space in the waiting room and let Shani sit, settling beside her with Bee on his lap. His face was beautiful in its tenderness. His faded shirt and loose jeans were an odd uniform for an angel of mercy, but Shani knew that when angels swooped to Earth, they sometimes left their wings at home. Grounded by their circumstances, they had no choice but to sit back and watch chaos unfurl. It was like a scene from Dante's Inferno being put on by the local grade school. Children sobbed, babies wailed, worried parents held them close or paced, gulping coffee, guzzling high-caffeine sodas and rooting around in greasy packets of potato chips. Half an hour passed, then half an hour more. Heads lifted whenever a new group of names rang out over the sound system. As each sick child's name was called, his or her parents left through the swinging doors leading into the guts of the building with a mixture of relief at finally making it inside and guilt at leaving fellow sufferers behind.

She needed to feel the warmth of her daughter against her skin and held out her arms wordlessly. Elliot handed Bee over and then stood to allow the blood to return to his legs. With a smooth movement, he pulled the damp, funky-smelling shirt over his head and tossed it onto the chair. He stroked his chest absently, looking down at himself. "Probably wouldn't pass dress code around here now," he commented in amusement.

She opened her mouth again, not even sure what she was going to say, and then shut it as the sight of his sleek, bare chest hit her between the eyes. The body he had on him certainly didn't belong on an angel; according to her understanding of the heavenly creatures, they wouldn't know what to do with it. The well-defined lines that accentuated his pecs, the glimpses of rib as he turned and abdominal muscles that plunged downward to the sharp angles of hip bones visible above his low-slung jeans were like the long, sleek lines of a sports car. She tried not to stare, but she lost the battle.

He shrugged the cricks out of his shoulder and snagged the next nurse to pass close enough. She was a fine-boned young Asian woman, probably not more than twenty-three or twenty-four, with straight black hair that escaped her little bonnet willy-nilly. Her large eyes were an unusual shade of deep green. As he stepped out into her path, she gave him a distracted glance—and then that glorious, golden expanse of bare chest stopped her in her tracks.

"Nurse, please. The baby's very sick, and her mother's worried. How long do you think it'll be?"

She swallowed, trying to keep her gaze above his neck. "We're very busy tonight—"

His voice was low, beguiling, betraying neither anger nor frustration. "I know you're all doing the best you can." He smiled disarmingly, one hand on her elbow, the other idly resting over his heart, like someone taking the Pledge of Allegiance—or declaring his affections. "But you look like a kind person. I'm sure you'd be willing to spare me a few seconds of your time."

Unconsciously, the young nurse lifted her fingers to her full, pink lips. Shani watched in amazement, feeling like Alice in some kind of soft-core Wonderland. *She looks as if she's willing to give a whole lot more time than a few seconds,* she thought.

"What I want to know is *why* is it so busy? This isn't normal, is it?"

The young woman lifted a stray strand of hair and tucked it behind her ear. She leaned forward, tiptoeing to get her mouth close to his ear, as if revealing an intimate secret. "It's not normal. Everything's gone crazy since they cut the budget."

"That so?"

"Mmm-hmm. They've reduced the staff on each shift."

"Even in the E.R.?"

She nodded. "We're two doctors and three nurses down tonight."

Elliot frowned. The hand that was idly playing over his chest fell to his side. "Don't they know the kind of suffering they're causing?"

She rolled her gorgeous green eyes and shrugged. "Money talks, I guess. The administrators aren't the ones here at two in the morning, having to deal with the mess they've created." She paused, mouth parted in anticipation, waiting on him to commend her for being a good girl.

His eyes held hers for several seconds longer than necessary. "Thank you, Nurse. I was right—you *are* very kind."

"Elena."

"Pardon?"

"My name. It's Elena. I'm on the graveyard shift every night until Wednesday. If you need anything…" She trailed off, not needing to draw him a diagram.

He released his light grip on her arm and took her hand instead, squeezing it lightly. "Thank you, Elena. I mean that."

"If I can slip you guys in a little earlier…well, I'll see what I can do." Elena gave her hair one final fluff and backed away, a little self-conscious, giving Shani one hard, curious look before turning and heading in the direction she'd come from.

"Surprised those scrubs didn't hit the floor," Shani murmured.

He sat next to her again. "What's that?"

"Nothing."

The smile he gave told her he'd heard exactly what she'd said.

But Elliot wasn't satisfied with waiting on little Miss Flirty-pants to fulfill her promise. He fished his phone from his pocket and scrolled one-handed through the numbers. He hit Dial and waited for the other person to answer, giving her a comforting smile.

Shani watched, amazed. Did he know what time it was?

"David, it's Elliot Bookman. Right. Junior. I'm guessing you're still at my father's party? Now breaking up, huh?" He waited. "How's my father? Well, he'll have a hell of a headache, that's for sure. Glad you and Maggie had a good time."

He cleared his throat. "Listen, David, I need a favor. I'm over at Immaculate Heart. In the E.R. No, it's a favor for a friend. We've got a three-year-old who needs to be seen, right away. Yes, I heard about the budget cuts. But the place is a mess. Think you could make a few calls? Maybe shift some of your staff over from another department? I'm sure it's quieter over in Medical tonight."

Shani tried not to shake her head. Even on the phone, he had a careless charm about him that appealed to both men and women. Did anyone ever tell him no?

He listened again, nodding. "That'd be great. Bless you,

man. Have a good night now, and take care on the road." He clicked off, smiling as though he'd won a game of chess.

She didn't bother trying to stifle her curiosity. "Who was that?"

"David Carmichael. He's on the board here. He and my father go way back. Anyhow, he's going to have a few more staff sent over. The bottleneck will clear up in a while."

He was right. In less than twenty minutes, Shani heard her name called. She rose with difficulty, Bee still deadweight in her arms, and turned to Elliot, preparing to thank him and wish him good-night. Already, a small shard of sadness pricked at her. All evening, he'd been as solid and reliable as a load-bearing wall. Now it was time to go in and face the thunder. What did you say to a stranger who helped you save the thing that means the most to you?

"Elliot, I…I don't know how to say thanks. I—"

"Let's go." He grabbed her by the elbow and began guiding her past the uneven rows of benches.

"What? Where're you—"

He gave her a surprised look. "Did you think I'd let you go in there alone?"

She protested. "I'm grateful for all you've done, but you really—"

He didn't stop walking. "Come on. They're waiting." He grabbed his shirt and tossed it over his shoulder like a towel.

There was no sense in arguing. As he held open the swinging doors, she took one guilty look at the sad people still waiting, sending up a prayer that their troubles would end soon.

Inside, an older nurse took up most of the entryway. Her expression was standard hospital-issue harassed, hair scraped back into a bun, face like a hatchet. She glanced at the proffered papers and nodded at a gurney. Shani set her burden down carefully, and at once an attendant began to work on Bee.

"You the mother?" The nurse asked.

"Yes."

"You can stay."

Shani moved to her daughter's side. Elliot moved in concert with her, only to be stopped by the nurse's imperious, uplifted hand. "Who're you?"

"My name's Elliot—"

She frowned, noticing for the first time that his chest was bare. Her eyes popped ceilingward in a "you-see-all-types-in-here" gesture, then she clarified. "I mean, what's your relationship to the patient? Only the parents of a minor are allowed in here."

"Oh, I—"

"So who're you?"

Shani found herself desperately wanting Elliot to stay with her in this awful place. "He's…he's…" She began and stopped.

The nurse, as intimidating as a mythical beast guarding treasure, folded her arms. What could she say to get this woman to understand? She half wondered if Elliot's charm could work on her, too. Bizarrely, even though it would mean his eviction and her abandonment, that almost made her feel satisfied. At least it would mean *someone* was immune to him.

Elliot hardly missed a beat. "I'm her father."

Shani choked on her own spit.

The nurse glanced at his face for half a second, then at Bee's damp, sallow one, and dismissed him with disinterest, pointing the way with her pen. The doors swung open behind them, admitting someone else for her to intimidate.

Shani felt Elliot close to her, warm skin occasionally

brushing her bare arm as they watched the doctor, an older black woman who reassuringly reminded her of Maya Angelou, fiddle with Bee. The woman gave her the first genuine smile she'd had since she got here.

"Don't worry, *doux-doux*. She ees going to be just fine." She spoke with an accent Shani couldn't identify. West African? Caribbean? "Just a leetle infection—nothing to make a whole lot of fuss and bother about. We'll start her on antibiotics right away. And just to be safe, we'll keep her for a few days, okay?"

Shani felt tears of gratitude and relief prickle at the backs of her eyes. The doctor patted her gently on the cheek. "Chin up, sugarplum. Don't you worry. She ees in good hands."

The doctor directed her gaze at Elliot's bare chest, and she asked humorously, "I know the cooling system needs fixing, but you don't think you taking thees a leetle too far?"

Elliot surprised Shani by looking abashed. "Sorry, Doctor. I apologize if I've offended…we had a little accident."

"Don't fret. I've seen it all." But Maya Angelou had the audacity to give him one last, evaluating glance. Elliot's skin flushed, and Shani hid a grin. It was like discovering your grandma's prayer-circle buddy was a flirt.

They followed Bee's gurney out of the E.R. and into a pediatric ward with three other beds. Gently, the attendant settled her onto the bed farthest from the door. With that movement, Bee's eyes shot open, startled, taking in the unfamiliar surroundings. "Mama?"

Shani was immediately soothing, stroking her cheek and listening to the sound of the monitors until she fell back into a heavy sleep. Only then did she look around. There were two armchairs next to each bed, and a little cabinet for personal effects. That was pretty much it. Children in the other beds were sleeping, their monitors a soft, bipping chorus, with the exception of a small, still pile of blankets two beds over, which was surrounded by anxiously whispering staff. A woman, probably the child's mother, hovered, trying to stand on tiptoe to see what they were doing. Shani sat in one of the chairs and closed her eyes briefly, not able to absorb anyone else's pain tonight.

She looked outside past lopsided blinds. It was clear and dark out, but she could tell there were only a few hours till dawn. She knew she wouldn't be sleeping.

"Hey."

Elliot squatted before her. He reached out and stroked her cheek, jolting her thoughts away from the window and the outside world. "She's a beautiful little girl," he said, but he was looking at Shani, not at Bee.

"Yes," she agreed, but her thoughts were not on Bee, either. Rather, they were focused on fighting the urge to lean her chin into his cupped hand. Where'd *that* come from?

Knowingly, he turned her face toward his. *Look away,* she told herself. *Look away, or you'll be turned to stone.* She couldn't, held fast by his dark stare. She heard machines around her whoop and beep, but she couldn't hear herself breathe.

"Hungry?"

"Wh…huh?" The banality of the question on the heels of such an intense connection left her flailing for a response.

To her disappointment, he rose. Easily, fluidly, like a snake uncoiling itself. "Gotta be a cafeteria in here somewhere. If I don't eat something soon…" He turned to go. "Coffee or tea?"

After having had nothing to eat since lunch, she figured

a meal would be worth not having him by her side for a bit. "Coffee, please."

"Sweet and milky, right?"

How'd he know? She watched him walk confidently away, beautiful chest bare to the world and not giving a damn. Her eyes remained fixed on him until he walked into the lit corridor. The only thing she could do now was try to catch a few moments' rest…and wait for him to come back.

Chapter 5

Shani's heart did a happy little two-step when he returned with a cardboard box lid and two hot cups of coffee balanced inside. He handed her a cup. It was sweet and milky, as promised. Comforting. He settled next to her with a grin, pointing to his bare chest. "Scared a few people out there."

"Uh-huh." More likely set their salivary glands going, she thought. "You cold?"

"Nah." He tilted the tray so she could see its contents. "Hot dogs. And pudding. They were out of chocolate—only butterscotch and banana left. Figured you'd like the butterscotch better."

"You figured right."

He handed her a hot dog, heavy on the ketchup and mustard, light on the relish, no onions. "They've been rolling around on that little carousel since the Jurassic, but I'm too hungry to complain."

She bit in. "If we get food poisoning, at least we're in the right place."

He smiled. "First joke I've heard you make all night."

She shrugged, concentrating on her hot dog. "Haven't got much to joke about."

She was disappointed when he didn't contradict her. He finished his hot dog without saying anything more. Then there was no sound but the scraping of his plastic spoon in the pudding cup. When she was done with hers, too, he whisked away the debris.

He snagged a blanket and wrapped it around his bare chest Indian-style, to deflect any more disapproving glances, and sat again. Together they listened to the sounds of the night. Outside, an ambulance wailed. Inside, a child moaned in his sleep. All underscored by the incessant chorus of instruments, like the mournful chirping of crickets. Eerie. Disturbing. Sad.

Elliot was so quiet, she was sure he'd dozed off. She was afraid to look at him, in case her anxiety, her need for him to stay awake, and stay with her, showed. It was embarrassing. Had she sunk so low that the moral support of a kindhearted stranger was all she had?

She directed her frustration and anger away from herself and onto Christophe. Jerk. He was an ocean away, not knowing, not caring that his daughter had loops of wires curling into and out of her, making her one with a huge, ugly machine. With just the glow of a monitor and the glimmer of a night-light staving off the darkness poised above her like a stilled wave.

How could he leave her alone to face this? When had he stopped loving her? She snorted derisively. To hear him tell it, he *did* still love her. Sleeping around throughout their marriage hadn't meant he didn't; it just meant he was

French. As far as he was concerned, she'd blown the whole thing out of proportion.

She exhaled, thinking of the envelope that lay on the floor in her apartment, waiting to be opened. She wondered if she'd ever have the strength. She'd certainly have the time, what with no longer being employed and all. She thought of how, not long ago, her dream job was hers, and money and status came with ease. She'd gone and made such a mess of things...

"It'll get better, you know." Elliot's mouth was close to her ear.

She jumped. Wasn't he asleep? She turned her startled eyes to him. "What?"

His voice was still soft, warm and gentle. "You sighed like something was breaking inside you. It hurt just to hear it. But it'll get better."

"How, Elliot? I lost my job—"

"—you'll get a better one."

"—my husband—"

"—if he deserved you, he'd be here instead of me—"

"And here alone, in this godawful place—"

"You're not alone," he pointed out.

She was too frustrated to acknowledge he was right. "—listening to my daughter breathe, depending on someone I've known *four hours* to be my savior!" Savior. His gaze was steady on hers, taking the appellation in stride, as though it belonged to him. She paused, panting. "Not that I'm ungrateful."

"I know—"

"You've gone out of your way—"

"Shani, stop—"

"No. You don't know anything about my life. But you sit there with this light in your eyes and tell me it's gonna get better? I'm sorry, Elliot. Forgive me if I don't believe—"

His kiss cut her tirade short. Both hands came up around her face, pulling her forward. The arms of their heavy chairs, jammed up against each other, made the gesture awkward, so without breaking the kiss he shifted around to kneel before her again, slipping one hand around her shoulders so she had no choice but to slide down off her chair and find herself knee to knee with him. Her short black waitressing skirt rode up on her thighs.

The blanket around his shoulders fell open, and his bare chest was warm against hers. She discovered the softness of his rumpled hair under her fingers. It was an aching, urgent kiss. Coffee-sweet. Banana pudding-sweet.

And in her mind, a jumble of words. *My God, I'm kissing this man. Someone warm under my hands after so long. Stubble under my fingers. He needs a shave…and a haircut. What's wrong with me? Tired. Hungry. Aching. Feel like I could fall into him and go to sleep, and know I'd be safe.*

She touched his face again. It was as warm as his chest, but wet. Wet? When he broke their kiss she heard and felt the air escape his lips, and then the sear of tears replaced the gentle pressure of his mouth. She put her hand up in shock, to rub off the smear on his face, knowing the tears were hers, not his. He was smiling. "I've had lots of reactions to a kiss, but I don't think crying was ever one of them."

"Oh, I…" She tried to wipe away the evidence with the back of her hand, but there was more where that came from. "Elliot, I'm so—"

"If I have to hear you say you're sorry one more time…!" He found a crumpled paper napkin and tried to mop up her face, but she took it from him.

"I can do it."

He didn't fight her. Instead, he stayed kneeling before

her, watching her soberly. When she was finished, he took the paper away, balled it up and sent it arcing into the wastepaper bin. "Better now?"

"I don't know."

"Come here." He pulled her head down against his chest. She complied without resistance. She could hear his heartbeat. She closed her eyes, listening to him breathe, and discovered to her surprise that his chest was rising and falling in tandem with the barely audible ins and outs of her daughter's breaths. She knelt in the arms of her personal angel, taking all the solace and comfort he offered. Wondering when he'd pull away and tell her to get up again.

He didn't. After a while, the silence was too much to bear. The holding, the warmth, were wonderful, but there was more she wanted. "Elliot?"

"Yes?" His voice was sonorous, muffled in her hair. Like a sound coming from far away.

"Tell me about yourself."

"I was born on a Sunday. My mother said it was raining…"

"That's not what I meant!" She looked up at him, seeing warmth and humor and awakening desire.

"How far back you want me to go?"

"Not that far. I just want to know something about you. This," she indicated their proximity, the intimacy of their positions facing each other. "This is so unlike me. I feel—"

"What do you feel?" He looked as though the answer was important to him.

She answered carefully, not willing to reveal too much. "I feel that…that it'd be less…weird…"

Another rumble of laughter, deep in his chest. "This feels weird to you?"

She was hesitant, not wanting to goad him to anger. "Well, a little. It's…unexpected."

"But sweet. Nice. The most natural thing…"

"I guess." She was a little doubtful. "But I feel… I think… It'd be a little less, you know…"

"Weird," he supplied indulgently.

"Yeah. That. If I knew more about you. I just met you. And now, this…"

"This is good."

Maybe. But it had been such a freaky night. She searched for a way to explain herself better.

She didn't have to. "But I get where you're coming from. What would you like to know?"

Now that the invitation was open, she pondered. What would she want to know? Ah, a question arose. The obvious question. "What's this thing between you and your father?"

He moved back an inch, but to her it was a chasm. "Anything but that."

So much for honesty. His reaction only piqued her curiosity more. What could be so bad that Elliot wouldn't even talk about it? Reluctantly, she conceded.

"What do you do when you're not rescuing sick little kids? And their mothers?" She glanced up at his windblown hair. "And riding a Triumph without a helmet?"

"Tech stuff. I'm an electronics engineer. My company designs information security systems." Now that Stack was no longer at the center of the conversation, he relaxed again, inching closer. "It's boring."

Boring was the last word she'd use to describe him. "Tell me something else."

"I can recite the alphabet backward. Want to hear it?"

She knew he was trying to make her smile. "Soon," she promised.

He wrapped her in the circle of his arms without seeking further permission. "I have the uncanny ability to sense when someone's hurting. When they need to be held."

Her eyelids lowered. Maybe that was all she needed to know right now.

He settled her down with her head in his lap, letting her curl up on the hard, cold hospital floor. "It'll be dawn in an hour or two. Get some rest. You'll need it when your daughter gets up."

She wasn't aware of anything more.

Chapter 6

Elliot let Shani sleep, even when the nurses made their dawn rounds to check Béatrice's vitals. Under the weight of her head, his legs didn't feel like his anymore, but that was okay. Letting her sleep gave him time to think.

What was he getting into? He'd done something rash last night, stealing Stack's car on the spur of the moment to help a stranger with a sick kid. He could live with that. If Stack wanted to kick his ass around the room afterward, so be it. Even hanging around with Shani last night was okay. It didn't hurt to give another human being a little support when she needed it.

But why was he still here? He'd fulfilled whatever tenuous duty he felt toward her; gotten her and the kid safely to the hospital, made sure they were attended to and even got her a halfway-decent meal. But the sun was up and the woman was asleep with her head on his lap. That was beyond the call.

And kissing her like that! The lady hadn't been divorced twenty-four hours, and he'd been all over her. Like a big dog rescuing a lame kitten, only to snap it up in one gulp the moment it thought it was home free. That's what you called letting your little head call the shots. It wouldn't happen again.

Shani stirred, opened her eyes sleepily, caught sight of him—and was jolted awake. In an instant she was kneeling upright, rigid. One hand covered her mouth. "Ohmigod!"

Not a reaction he was used to coming from any woman who'd ever slept within two feet of him. "What?"

"I slept on you! I must have been asleep for hours. Oh, Lord, I hope I didn't drool." She rubbed at her face like a hamster.

"Not a whole lot."

"Oh, Elliot… Did I give you cramps? In your legs, I mean."

"Uh, yeah." He rose painfully, hearing his knees creak. "But with a little therapy, I'll be able to walk again." She cringed, forcing him to pat her lightly on the cheek. "Kidding. Don't worry, I'll be fine."

Then he had the pleasure of seeing her fingers rise to her lips again as she remembered their kiss. Watching her color up, evidence of how much she'd enjoyed it, made him feel less predatory. Maybe calling a moratorium on kissing her had been a tad hasty….

Shani went quickly to her daughter's bedside, anxiety wiping away the memory of last night's pleasurable interlude. That piqued him some, but women were women: their kids always came first. He gave his ego a kick in the pants and hurried to join her.

"Nurses passed by while you were asleep—"

"Why didn't you wake me up?"

"No need. The whole thing went down in about ninety seconds. They checked her vitals—she's down to one-oh-one—and said she was doing fine. She'll sleep for a while, though."

"Still, you could've—"

"You were tired."

She touched her hair, which had abandoned any pretense of being in a bun, and now fell to the tops of her shoulders. He liked the way it looked, all chestnutty and mussed. He resisted the urge to touch a strand.

"Do I look tired? My face isn't creased, is it? God, I must be a mess." She bent over to yank her skirt down over her well-shaped butt, giving him a shot all the way down the top of her dress. "This thing's riding up on me like Paul Revere. Damn Yvan and his stupid tight uniforms."

Bless Yvan and his tight uniforms, he thought, but was too smart to say it out loud. He watched her finger-comb her hair and smooth herself down, a little feminine vanity that made him feel flattered. She wanted to make herself presentable, sure, but he knew that there was also a kernel of desire to look good for him. Nice. "You look fine. But if it'd make you feel better, why don't you let me take you back home so you can have a quick shower and change?"

She looked at him as if he'd blasphemed. "I'm not leaving here until my daughter does."

"Which won't be for another day or two," he reminded her.

She shrugged. "Then I'll just have to walk around looking like I slept in a cardboard box."

He didn't try to dissuade her, but he offered an alternative. "Well, they've got hospitality rooms where parents can go have a shower and change. How 'bout I run over to your place and pick you up some fresh clothes?"

She looked doubtful, even though the prospect of clean clothes was sweet. "I don't know…"

"You don't have to let me root through your private stuff. Why not call your sitter…" He searched for her name.

"Gina?"

"Right. Why not call Gina, have her pack a bag for you and Béatrice, and then I'll bring it for you?"

The tempting offer found its mark. "You'd do that?"

"Sure."

She frowned slightly, eyes searching his face. "Why?"

Good question, but he didn't have an answer. He shrugged.

"That would be…very kind. I'll call her." She fished around in her bag for her phone.

Speaking of the need for a shower, he was getting a little pungent himself. He handed her his card. "If you need anything else, call. I'll go home now. Catch some shut-eye, maybe. Then I'll swing by later with your stuff. Need breakfast before I go?"

"Thanks, but I can sneak away before she wakes up and get a sandwich in the cafeteria."

He smiled, remembering last night's hot dog, which still resided somewhere behind his breastbone. "Good luck with that. I'll bring you lunch. Anything you don't eat?"

"No, I eat pretty much everything." She rolled her eyes and added, "'Cept maybe liver."

"That never entered my mind." He tossed aside his makeshift toga and found his shirt, a stinky ball of fabric that was taking on a life of its own in a corner. "You'll be all right till I get back?"

"I'll be fine." The resolution in her voice was as much for her own reassurance as for his.

"Good. Won't be gone long." He hesitated. Now that he was leaving, how should he say goodbye? A handshake hardly seemed appropriate. He'd kissed her, long and hard, mere hours ago. Should he...? No. He'd promised himself. That would be like shooting fish in the shallow end of the pond.

She seemed to be wondering the same thing. She swallowed hard. "Elliot..."

He brushed her cheek with the backs of his fingers and all but ran out of there.

Chapter 7

"One fish, two fish," Elliot was saying.

"Red fish, blue fish!" Bee finished and yowled with delight. Shani watched as he perched on the edge of Bee's bed and read from her favorite Dr. Seuss book…or, rather, as she constantly interrupted him to parrot passages she'd memorized. He was doing a decent job of sounding fascinated, even as he heard the story of Ned and his little bed for the eighth time.

The connection between the two had been instant, which was odd. Not that Bee had taken to him so easily. She was a friendly child. What was odd was the ease with which *Elliot* had taken to *Bee*. While most men his age shied away from kids as though they were buggier than an anthill, he unleashed upon her the same easy, engaging charm he used on everyone else. From the first day, Bee had literally been eating out of his hand.

As Shani approached, Elliot looked up with a smile. "Your daughter's reading to me."

"I'm reading to him, Mama!"

"So I see." Shani smiled and fiddled with Bee's discharge papers, folding and unfolding them. She had the awkward sense that she was intruding. She and Bee had been quietly cuddling, singing nursery rhymes. When Elliot turned up, Bee had abandoned Shani's lap and bounded over to him. That irked her a little.

Elliot spotted the papers in her hand. "All set?"

"Yes. She's ready." The ordeal was over. All she wanted to do was go home.

Elliot got to his feet. "Packed?"

She pointed at the black duffel bag on the armchair. "That's all of it."

Elliot picked up the bag and tossed it onto his shoulder.

Shani turned to Bee, who still had the book open on her lap but who had stopped reading and was intently following the conversation. "It's time to go home, sweetheart. Why don't you put that book away."

The little face screwed up into an obstinate scowl, the kind every parent recognizes and dreads. "No. I'm reading to Elliot."

"I know you are, sweetie, but we have to go."

"I'm reading for Elliot! I need to tell him the one about… the…the…" She struggled, flipping through the pages for a story that was sure to win her a few minutes. "The one with the Zack, and the Gack, and the…"

Shani tried to be at once soothing and firm. "Elliot's already heard them, Bee. But we have to leave. The nice doctor said you can go."

"But I don't wanna!" Tears threatened to spill.

Like I really need this, Shani thought. She went into do-as-I-say mode. "Listen, Bee, we're going, and that's—"

"But I wanna stay with Elliooot!" Her anguished, obstinate face looked like a crumpled ball of paper.

Shani understood. Bee thought Elliot came with the hospital. As she moved to explain, Elliot cut her off. "I don't live here, Bee."

The rebellious scowl softened. "You don't?"

He smiled easily, indulgently. "'Course not. I came here just to see you."

"Me?"

He gave Shani a loaded glance. "And your mama."

Shani kept her eyes deliberately on Bee's face.

Elliot was still talking, softly, steadily, like someone trying to charm a small animal that had backed itself into a corner but was willing to bite its way out. "I'm here to give you guys a ride home."

That was enough for the crumpled ball of paper to smooth itself out, transforming into a smile again. "In your car?"

"In my car. You'll like it."

"Can my Mama come?"

Again, that long look over Bee's head, the kind that said things children weren't supposed to hear. "'Course, she can come. She can sit up front, right next to me."

That was all Bee needed to hear. She bounded down from the bed. "My shoes! Mama, hurry!"

Shani found them and dropped to her knees to help her put them on, glad for the distraction. As much as she was relieved to be out of this place, she couldn't help but share a little of Bee's reluctance to go. The hospital, and her position of need, were the only things that linked her to Elliot. He'd been a pillar for her, and as much as she couldn't fully understand why, she'd been too tired to argue.

But soon she'd be home again, standing on her two feet. Back to taking care of her daughter and facing some difficult career decisions. She wouldn't need him anymore. Once he was done with the Cub-Scout-good-deed-a-day routine, would she see him again?

She thought of their kiss. Every day, when he came to drop her stuff off, he'd hung around awhile, playing cards, divvying up the newspaper and making idle chat over the boxed meals he brought. But never once did he show any sign of bringing his lips to hers again. Sometimes, to her chagrin, she'd sat there next to him as Bee slept, murmuring responses as he chattered on, and all the while a single silent command radiated outward from her: *kiss me again, kiss me again, kiss me again…* It didn't seem as if he ever heard it.

Her thoughts preoccupied her as Bee was wheeled to the hospital exit—making engine noises all the way—and deposited on the front step. Shani squinted in the bright afternoon light. She hadn't been outside since Bee had been admitted. They began meandering through the parking lot, looking for Elliot's car.

"Lookmamalookmamalook!" Bee was chanting. Elliot had his right arm bent, and Bee was hanging like a monkey from the crook of it, both feet off the ground, being carried along as they walked by the power of his flexed biceps.

She protested. "You're too big for that! Get down!"

"It's fine," Elliot assured her.

"Bee! You put your feet down and walk, this instant!"

"It's fine, Shani," he repeated quietly.

Her irritation at being contradicted was softened by the amused contentment on his face. Elliot was enjoying the little game, shuffling along, making gorilla noises and rolling his eyes as though it took his very last shred of strength to haul around Bee's thirty-five-pound frame. They'd made friends, he and her daughter.

That was both delightful and disturbing. Bee had been through so much not having her father around. Christophe hadn't lived with them in over two years. To see her brimming with hope and excitement every time he turned up for one of his hit-and-run visits, and then to deal with the weeks of anguish and acting-out that followed his departure, were as much as she could bear. Elliot was just passing through. Was it really a good idea to let her get attached?

It wasn't hard to spot Elliot's car, an Italian beast that could only have been a custom job. Given that he'd already demonstrated an affinity for fast, expensive vehicles, she'd been willing to bet it would have been a low-slung, two-door road monster. What she hadn't seen coming was the custom paint job, a pearlescent dusky rose, a shade of pink that had almost erotic connotations. She couldn't hold back a grin. The man was so confident in his masculinity he could paint his car pink and get away with it.

Bee was as impressed. "Ooh! It's pink, Mama! Look!"

"I see."

She gave Elliot a happy smile. "Pink's my favorite color." That was news to Shani. Up to several seconds ago yellow-and-black bee stripes had held that place of honor.

He allowed Bee to uncurl herself from around his forearm, gave one last gorilla grunt and set her down. Then he threw the duffel in the trunk and let Bee climb in. Shani was about to get in after her, to hold her in her arms on the ride home, when she spotted a red car seat. She gave Elliot a questioning look.

He lifted his shoulders. "Didn't want her driving across town in the middle of the day without a seat belt."

He'd bought Bee a car seat for a single trip? "So you spent money on a—"

"It cost next to nothing. Relax." He reached over and buckled Bee in, and that was the end of that. Shani got into the front passenger seat and as he buckled her in, his hands were quick and efficient. But his eyes, holding hers, existed within their own slow-motion universe.

The trip back to Catarina allowed enough time for Shani to mull over her predicament. Bee's incessant chirping and Elliot's amused murmurs of reply ensured she wouldn't be called upon to contribute to the conversation.

The storefronts and buildings reflected in her window were hardly what she'd call run-down, but they did have a little age on them. Shani liked them; they were noisy, slightly overcrowded, busy and…happy. Catarina was a happy place, full of quaint little stores and ethnic restaurants, and the streets were always full of people, even at night.

But it was a far cry from where she'd come. Most of the time, she didn't miss her former life, the one with the high-rise at the heart of Santa Amata, the apartment with the doorman and concierge. The time in her life when she didn't have to worry about money.

Going back to that life would be fairly simple. A few phone calls, maybe a letter, would be all it took. But simple didn't mean easy. She was sure if she tried to pick up where she'd left off before Christophe had sideswiped her complacent, unruffled existence, she'd fail, and her bruised self-esteem wouldn't be able to take it. How could she ever be good at her old job again? Hell, she couldn't even keep a job waitressing!

Once Elliot pulled up outside her apartment they all

hopped out, but Bee never made it upstairs. The doors of Old Seoul were thrown open and out ran Gina Pak, with her mother in close pursuit. Bee launched herself into their arms, a cannonball of energy.

"Too thin! Too thin!" Mrs. Pak admonished, her bony hands encircling Bee's tiny wrist. She was as aghast as if Bee had been stowed away in a cellar for a month.

"I told you they don't feed them in the hospital, Oma," Gina said to her mother. She clucked like a woman several times her age.

"Hospital food!" Mrs. Pak spat out her disgust. "No good. Come, baby. We have *kimchi*. And *miyuk gook*. Good for you. Better than medicine." Mrs. Pak gave Shani a firm look. "We taking her. She needs food."

Shani didn't bother to protest. With Gina exclaiming in English and her mother murmuring endearments in Korean, Bee was carried aloft as if she were a basketball player who'd clinched the game with nine seconds to the final whistle.

Before the door closed, Gina stopped to yell. "We'll keep her for the afternoon, Shani. Elliot told me you weren't getting any sleep. Go on, get some rest." She gave Elliot a knowing look. "You need some alone time, dontcha?" Her head disappeared and the door slammed shut before Shani could protest the implication behind Gina's statement.

Elliot looked amused. "Does your daughter have any idea what they're going to feed her in there? You know *miyuk gook* is seaweed, right?"

Shani shrugged. "If I try to feed her seaweed, I'll be wiping it up off the floor. If the Paks feed it to her, she'll be asking for seconds."

Then the doors to the restaurant flew open again, and Gina's glossy head poked through.

"Elliot, I kept the…um…thing…" She gave Shani a look

she couldn't decipher. "The present. We kept it here until Bee got back. She's playing with it now."

Shani pricked up her ears. Present? For her daughter? What kind of present could Gina have to keep for them until Bee got home? She tried to catch Elliot's attention, but he was focused on Gina, smiling as if it was Christmas and he'd been appointed interim Santa while the real one took the day off. "Did she like it?" he asked.

Gina rolled her eyes. "Are you kidding me?" Then the disembodied head was gone.

Elliot took her elbow. "Come. Gina's right. You need some rest."

She walked with him, curiosity killing her. "What present?"

He looked sheepish. "Just a little something I picked up for her on the way over. An impulse buy. A homecoming present."

She didn't like the sound of that. "Cough it up, or I'm heading back downstairs to see for myself. What kind of present?"

He waited until she kicked the front door shut and followed her into the hallway before admitting, "The kind that meows."

She nearly dropped her keys. "You mean the *toy* kind that *pretend* meows."

He shook his head slowly. "I mean the real kind that honest-to-God meows."

"You mean the kind that scratches the furniture and craps on the rug?"

"I got it a litter box and a scratching post. And a whole bunch of dry food, wet food, treats." He moved to stand in front of her and let the duffel fall to the floor. He was smiling at her, that smile that could charm the scales off a snake. "I got it toys, a little bed—"

"You got my kid a cat?"

"Kitten."

"Newsflash—they grow up. You got my kid a cat without asking me?"

"I know, I should have asked. But I was driving by a pet shop, and I went in on impulse. I just wanted her to have something nice to come home to after that terrible experience."

If he thought she was going to let him stand there and insult her, he was out of his damn mind. "Oh, so our home isn't something nice to come home to?"

"That's not what I meant. I meant I wanted her to have a nice surprise…"

"You could have got her ice cream. Or a doll that pees." She wanted to punch him for his thoughtlessness. She turned away from him before she got herself in trouble—and caught sight of the envelope that had shaken her world. It was lying on the floor, right where she'd tossed it. She picked it up and looked at it, temporarily distracted.

Elliot was at her shoulder, protesting, confessing, placating. "I know I should've asked—"

"Yeah, you should've."

"I was just afraid you'd say no."

She dragged her eyes away from the letter to his. "That was the point of asking. What if I hate cats?"

"You don't."

"And how do you know that?"

He pointed at the keys dangling from her fingers. "There's a brass cat on your key ring, for one." He pointed at the pale lemon walls. "You've got a charcoal drawing of a cat there, and another over there. Look around you, Shani…"

She did. The living room was as neat as it could be, given that a toddler was in residence; there was a couch and love seat, and a deep orange marmalade area rug that brought cheer to the place and lifted the yellow of the walls. The walls were adorned with paintings from Martinique and a large framed photo showing fishing *pirogues* drawn up on the sand waiting for high tide. Christophe had taken that, blown it up for her as a present. Her reading corner was furnished with a white rattan rocking chair and coffee table set, also from Martinique, and a birch bookcase crammed with books, photos of herself and her daughter…and a cat-shaped candle holder. She didn't have to look beyond the living room to know he could see the dining table which had, at its center, a slightly cheesy flowerpot rimmed with playing kittens.

His grin was all victory. "That's how I know."

She stood her ground. "All the same, you can't just walk in here with a living, breathing animal…another responsibility to rest upon my shoulders, without asking…." She rubbed her thumbs along the seal of the envelope in her hands, reading again the return address of her lawyer: *Dorian Black, Attorney at Law…* "I've got a lot going on in my life…" Her protests faded as her thoughts were reabsorbed by the contents of the envelope.

"You don't need to open that right now." Elliot was behind her, comforting and concerned. She didn't need him to be.

She didn't need his advice, either. She opened the envelope anyway, carefully, slowly, trying to ease up the flap without tearing it. As though she didn't want the real owner to know she'd been prying. She withdrew the heavy papers inside and read them, taking a long time, as if it was written in a foreign language that she'd studied way back in school and was a little rusty. She tried to replace them just as carefully, unwilling to crease them, but her hands were shaking too much.

Elliot took the papers from her and slid them into the envelope, not even trying to catch a glimpse of their contents. He set them down. "You okay?"

Okay? With her lungs compressing the way they were? "I need air," she gulped.

"Want to take a walk? We could—"

She brushed past him, almost running over to the other side of the apartment, out onto a small patio. The air was fresh and stinging. She closed her hands over the railing. She tried not to listen to the traffic sounds from outside and the general hubbub of the restaurant below. Instead, she fine-tuned her ear to pick up the soothing rustle of the wind through the rows of potted plants that lined the balcony and brushed her knees. The pots were filled with herbs and vegetables: lettuce, cabbages and tomatoes.

Elliot's voice was close. "You've got a green thumb."

She glanced down to the plants at her sides. They were as healthy, lush and leafy as she'd left them, probably thanks to Gina watering them while she was away. Bless the girl. Heavy tomatoes weighed down their plants, since she hadn't been around in days to pick them. She shrugged. "Least I know they're pesticide free."

He picked a few of the ripest, sweetest-looking tomatoes and placed them in a small straw basket she kept there for that purpose. "I admire people who can make things grow."

She was too absorbed in her own frustration and helplessness to respond. Her life was such a mess she didn't know where to start cleaning it up, and he was blabbing on about her damn tomatoes? She wished he'd leave her to her misery. She'd *make* him leave her to it. She spun around and fixed him with her best glare. "Listen, Elliot. I don't want to sound ungrateful. I'm thankful for all you've done for my family. You were there when we needed you. But I'm home now, and Bee's fine. I'm fine…"

He folded his arms, his face giving nothing away. When she fished for more to say, he prodded her gently. "So…?"

"So maybe you should leave me be. Don't you ever work?"

He shrugged. "I own the place. I work on my own schedule. Besides, I thought you'd need the company."

"I don't. And I don't need you to pick my damn tomatoes. And I sure as hell don't need you bringing my daughter cats!"

His mouth curved. He lifted a single finger. "One cat."

"You think this is funny? Stop playing around with me. I don't need you. I don't need any present-bringing guy hanging around and…and—" She was almost hyperventilating. Why couldn't she get him to—

Both his large hands were at her back, and she found herself pressed against the balcony behind her. For a dizzying second she was afraid she'd topple over it if she tried to escape. But he was so intoxicatingly warm, and so close…why would she want to? She was trapped, in his arms and in his gaze.

"You're not mad about that cat," he informed her with certainty.

"I sure in hell am mad about—"

"Or the tomatoes, or anything else you'd like to pretend."

She snorted. "And you know that."

"I know that."

"So, what am I mad about? The deficit?"

One corner of his mouth quirked ironically. "Probably

not that either, maddening as it is. You're mad at me because it's been three days…" He edged closer.

She didn't like where this was going. "What are you—?"

"Three long days…" That full mouth, with its mocking smile, was closer still. Too close.

"Elliot, you'd better not try—"

"Since I kissed you," he whispered into her ear.

She sputtered. "What? You think I—"

"I know you want me to. I see it every time you look at me. When you think I'm not looking." He brushed his lips against hers, but he took them away before her brain could process the significance of the contact. "Sometimes, I turn around and catch you. With that little puzzled frown. And I know you're thinking—" he did a reasonable imitation of a female voice "—why isn't he making a move? Why doesn't he kiss me again?"

That was outrageous! She hauled back and gave him the punch on the shoulder he'd been angling for ever since he got here. It didn't even rock him, but it startled him enough to allow her to slip past and dart back into the safety of her living room. "Get out, Elliot. I mean it."

"No, you don't."

"Yes, I do." She was throwing him out and making sure her door was well and properly locked. "Geez, man, why're you…why don't you…" Then her lips had better things to do.

God, he tasted good. Her mind lurched back to that kiss on the hospital floor and the tender, comforting feel of it. It had been the kind of kiss that soothed away her fears, acknowledged her anxieties and offered her a place to rest and refuel her tired soul.

This was not that kind of kiss. It was raw and lusty and raunchy. It sent shock waves down her spine and into her shoes, up into her hair, so intense she didn't dare open her eyes. It sent a web of tingles across the surface of her skin, a hundred fiery darts of excitement and sensation. It was the kind of kiss, if they'd let it go on, that the sun could have dropped out of the sky and she wouldn't notice.

He broke it and looked down at her, victory—and lipstick—coloring his grin. "If you don't want this, I can stop."

He was angling for another punch. She'd aim for the mouth, but that would be doing herself no favors. She wondered how to reply.

He didn't give her the chance. "Over here. Now." With one arm around her waist, he all but dragged her caveman-style over to her couch, whisked her up and plunked her onto it. He swung a leg over her hip and stretched out, cradling her head with one hand. And he kissed her again, even harder. Even longer.

He lifted his head again. "Like I said, if you want me to stop…"

With the full length of him upon her, the weight of him, she was having trouble thinking in coherent sentences, much less speaking in them. "Hate you when…when… right."

He laughed.

Her fingers were tangled—literally tangled—in his dark, unruly hair. The messy thatch made a useful handhold. She grabbed herself a bunch and yanked his head down to hers. "Ouch," he protested against her mouth.

"Then for God's sake…get yourself…go cut it."

"Sure." His tongue roamed her throat. "But in the meantime, feel free to—" he groaned in pleasure "—to pull on it some more."

She reveled in the weight of him, the determination and curiosity with which he pulled at the buttons of her shirt and bared her shoulders and the tops of her breasts, shifting slightly to allow him access to the clasp of her bra. When it was off, he buried his face between her breasts, stroking her from armpit to hip, inhaling her scent as if he wanted to fill himself with it.

She tried not to listen to the questions buzzing in the remaining logical part of her mind, the last holdout against the rebellion of sensation that was taking over. Questions like *What the hell are you doing?* and *Are you crazy?*

"Now you know." His voice was muffled in the fullness of her flesh.

"Wha—" Oh *man*, what he was doing felt good!

He lifted his head from the valley in which it was nestled, pupils wide and black with desire. "Now you know why I didn't kiss you at the hospital. I was afraid if I did, we wouldn't be able to stop. Didn't want to get thrown out onto the sidewalk…"

"We wouldn't have…gone this far…"

He shrugged as if he didn't believe her. "We got this far pretty fast." The amused, sensual smile that had lit his face from within dimmed slightly. He sighed and shifted, allowing her to sit up. He rubbed his head as if she'd punched him there, rather than on the shoulder. "Actually, getting dumped out onto the sidewalk wasn't the only thing I was scared of. I thought it might be…this might be…too fast for you. Given your circumstances."

"Given the fact that I've been divorced less than a week, you mean?" she asked wryly.

"That, yes. *Am* I moving too fast?"

She scrunched up her brow. How fast was fast? "How'm I supposed to answer that?" She was single again. Free. She could get involved with anyone she chose. She thought of Christophe. She didn't owe him her loyalty anymore. She didn't owe him access to her body anymore, even though she'd given of it freely every time he'd breezed through to visit his daughter. Even when the divorce proceedings were at their height.

That had always been her curse, her Achilles' heel. Her body's weakness for her husband and his expert lovemaking. Even though she knew he'd honed those skills in the beds of other women, many of them during their marriage. He was capable of filling her up, over and over, all the while making her want more and more and more. And when he left her, he left her still hungry.

Maybe that was what this was about; this sudden and inexplicable sexual longing for a man she barely knew, but who was too attractive and too kind. Residual hunger, the ferocious longing that Christophe had raised within her and left chained to a dungeon wall when he went away. What if...?

What if she let that longing loose?

Elliot was searching her face for an answer, his frustration evident when he found none. "Want to talk about it?"

She shook her head emphatically. "No."

He looked both disappointed and relieved. "What do you want to do, then?"

She closed her eyes to shut him out, wanting to be alone in her dilemma. He wasn't her type; rich, reckless, overconfident...and she was pretty sure she wasn't his. But that didn't matter, if all she wanted was a distraction. Escape.

He was gorgeous; she'd seen him naked from the waist up, and it didn't take a psychic to know that he'd be equally glorious from the waist down. He kissed like an incubus, and she knew deep in her hot, achingly aroused core that he'd make love like one, too. So why not? Why not lose herself in him, take what he was offering, gorge herself on him until she felt better? Maybe it'd be a one-night stand, maybe a twofer, maybe it'd last a month before he got bored and returned to the giddy little socialites she was sure he was used to. He wouldn't expect more. She shouldn't, either.

She was balanced on a tightrope, and either way she turned, she'd fall. Stay. Go away. Stay. She discovered he was holding her hand.

"Is the front door locked?" she asked.

Chapter 8

Winnie the Pooh got an eyeful that afternoon. In the apartment's only bedroom, which Shani shared with her daughter, the little potbellied bear looked down from his poster onto the bed, a silly grin on his face. She was glad that, being a bear of very little brain, he didn't have the noodle to understand what was going on.

Elliot was a sexual tornado, a whirling sandstorm that almost stripped her skin with its intensity. Finesse be damned; they'd bounded onto the bed, stripped off and paused for exactly nine and a half seconds to allow him to get his condom out of his wallet and onto him. After that, it was no holds barred.

His hands didn't stop. He explored her, curious and intrigued. His tongue was a fine blade that cut strips of sensation across her skin so intense she once caught herself looking down at her torso to see if she was bleeding. Licking her in the most surprising places: in the crook of her elbow, at the pulse point of her wrist, along her sternum as if tracing the line of the rib cage that lay beneath.

He tortured her nipples with the abrasive sandpaper of his stubble until the thin, blood-engorged skin was painfully excited, every tiny pore taut and erect. He sought out moles and childhood scars about her body, his tongue lingering over every irregularity like a high-definition scanner memorizing the details of the moon's surface.

As she pulled on his too-long hair to guide his head where she wanted it, she wondered briefly if telling him to get it cut had been a mistake. There was no denying; it came in handy.

And then playtime was over. A guttural sound emanating deep from his throat was his only signal that he was as ready as she. He rose to his knees, making assumptions about her flexibility she wasn't sure she could fulfill: looping her ankles up over his shoulders as he positioned himself above her. He didn't ease into her, slide in or glide in. Penetration was sharp, swift and complete, filling her up so suddenly it was almost an assault, an invasion that destroyed her defenses and blew any remaining resistance out of the water. Elliot had staged a coup on her body, and the logic that governed it gave up without so much as a token resistance.

Then she felt a sharp pain at the base of her spine, which intensified with every powerful thrust. "Oh, ow!"

He answered with an obscene endearment, a challenge to stay the course with him, not breaking his stroke.

The pain was too insistent. She writhed, but was unable to pull away, since she was staked to the bed by his body like a tent held down by a wooden peg. "Ow. Ouch, Elliot!"

He stopped this time, his fever-flushed face registering

concern. "Too rough? I thought you'd like it like this…I…"

"No, I…I do…it's not…" He got it wrong. Rough was wonderful; the abrasion was just what she needed. Scouring away her loneliness, filling a void. No moonlight and roses. No soul kisses, no Ne-Yo on the radio. This was good. What was hurting her had nothing to do with him. She contorted her body so she could slide her hand under her back, no small task with her legs still wrapped around him.

He was frowning. "Then what…should I…" He moved to withdraw.

Over her dead body. She stayed him with her other hand. "You move, you die," she threatened. She pulled the culprit out from under her back. It was a small bee-shaped windup toy, one of the many companions Bee insisted on sleeping with. She showed it to him and then tossed it to the floor. "Occupational hazard," she commented. She pressed her spine against the mattress, making sure there were no more intruders tangled in the sheets. "Proceed."

He gave her an almost formal nod. "Ma'am." And the battle resumed with its original intensity.

Shani closed her eyes, head tilted back, swamped by sensation. How long had it been? Four months? Five? The last time Christophe had done his bad-penny trick, she'd been as mad at him as she always was, as unwilling to forgive his transgressions as she had been the day she'd filed for divorce, but, God help her, the moment Bee had fallen asleep in this room she and her soon-to-be ex had set her living room sofa on fire.

Miserable jerk. She'd always been a woman who enjoyed sex, and in her single days she wasn't beyond indulging in the pleasure for its own sake, but there was something different about Christophe. With his island-grown Caribbean good looks and French mannerisms, he'd sucked her in like a carnal black hole.

Before she'd met him, she'd thought of her sexuality as a small but feral cat, capable of seeking out what it wanted and scratching if it needed to. But with Christophe feeding her desire, it had grown into a tigress so ferocious it needed to be kept on a leash.

And now, slick with Elliot's sweat, and with hers, she heard it roar, from deep within the dungeon where she'd confined it. With her fingers buried in the flesh of his hips, demanding he do the impossible—go even deeper, thrust even harder—she felt it snap its chains. The sleek wild animal was loose, its muscles bunched as it was about to leap, pounce on her and devour every rational thought… and it scared the hell out of her.

With orgasm so close she could already feel its approach, Shani panicked. This was lust, pure and wonderful. Every molecule in her body wanted her to fall headlong over the precipice, to collapse onto the cushion of forgetfulness at its base. But lust meant trouble. Once upon a time, it had bamboozled her, blinded her until she was so entangled with Christophe she couldn't find a way out. Now it was going to get her into trouble with Elliot, too.

The tigress was checked in midpounce. As it found itself bound by the chains it had sought to escape, it let out a roar of frustration, which was choked off in its throat. Shani felt her body go cold.

But Elliot, also teetering on the brink, waiting for her, couldn't stop himself, and he fell into the abyss with an exhalation that rocked his body. Shani watched his face intently, captivated by the grimace that smoothed into an expression of peace and fulfillment. Then her incubus was an angel again; damp, yes, fallen, certainly, but still her angel. He eased off of her, onto the bed at her side, unwilling to release her. He closed his eyes as she smoothed his thick, unruly brows, traced the shape of his ear.

He encircled her wrist and brought her hand down between them, pressing her fingers against his chest so she could feel the pounding of his heart. Then he reached out and rested his hand flat against her breast, absorbing the soft thudding of her own heartbeat. As she'd been unwilling, unable to make that final leap, it was far steadier than his.

The satisfaction on his face was disturbed by puzzlement, like the wake of a skier across an otherwise placid lake. "What happened? You were right there. I thought we were…doing this together."

She turned her face slightly, away from his. Above them, her daughter's bee mobile spun idly, fanned by the heat they'd generated. It hadn't been his fault; he'd done everything she'd wanted him to, and more. She didn't want to see his confusion.

"Shani?"

She could smell his sense of failure at not having taken her where he'd gone. He'd think it was his fault. How could she tell him he was wrong? "Nothing happened."

"Nothing? That was nothing?" He sat up and groaned. "Oh, for Pete's sake, look at me. You owe me at least that."

He was right. She paid her debt, not having the strength to sit up as well, but twisting so he could look down into her face. "It wasn't you."

"Glad to hear it. What was it, then?"

"It doesn't concern you."

He was incredulous. "Doesn't concern me? I'm naked. You're naked. We've been going at it like monkeys for the last—" he checked his watch "—hour. You go cold on me seconds before the finish line—"

"It wasn't a race."

He clicked his tongue impatiently. "You know what I mean. And you're telling me it doesn't concern me?"

She couldn't decide if he looked more hurt or insulted. Both were bad. The curse of the tigress was already manifesting. "God, I wish we'd never—"

"Don't say what I think you're going to," he begged. "Don't make me hate myself for this. It's not fair."

He was right. It wasn't fair to leave him feeling like that, especially since he'd done nothing to cause it. She reached up and ran her hand along his arm. The muscles tensed. She let her hand fall. "Elliot, I don't want to hurt you..."

"Then talk to me."

She was stuck in quicksand. She could stay still and drown slowly, or she could thrash about and drown fast. Might as well thrash about. "Like I said, it wasn't about you. It's just that when I was with Christophe—"

"Your husband?"

"—*ex*-husband—"

"You were thinking about him? Oh, man!" He levered himself off the bed and stalked toward the bathroom.

She rushed to reassure him. "Not that way!"

He got rid of the condom, put back on his undershorts and jeans and splashed water on his face before answering. "Not what way?"

"Not the way you think."

The face that had been so open to her minutes before, letting her see every flicker of pleasure, was on lockdown. His eyes were steady, unwavering and very black. "How do you know what I'm thinking?"

"You're stomping off, looking like I just told you I used you as a human sex toy, and you want to know how—"

"Well, did you?"

"No!"

"'Then tell me what the damn problem is!" he bellowed.

She stood before him, cutting off his escape from the bathroom, arms folded across her breasts. He had the advantage of being clothed; she'd never felt more naked. "I panicked."

His voice was a little gentler. "Why?"

How to explain? "I...really like sex," she began.

He almost smiled. "So do I."

"I mean, I really, really do..."

This time, he did smile. "You say that like it's a bad thing."

"Depends."

"On?"

"On where it leads you. For me, it led straight to Christophe. And look at what *that* brought me."

She could sense the anger leaking out of him. He rubbed her arms encouragingly. "If you tell me about it, it'd help me understand. You'd feel better, too."

She doubted it, but she bit the bullet anyway. "I met him in Martinique. I was only supposed to be there for a few weeks, doing research for a history project. Slavery in the French Caribbean, the *nègres marrons* and all that..." She stopped. That was another story. One she didn't need to get into.

Naturally, Elliot caught the slip. "History project?"

She shook her head. "Never mind. It's a long story."

"Then we'll save it for another time," he said firmly. "Go on."

"He was a photographer. He knew a lot about the island. He knew people who could help me. I went to him for an interview, and, well, I made the classic mistake—I fell for a charming man with a foreign accent and a silver... *lying* tongue. It was partly the island, you know, the sun and the sand. The rum punch…" She laughed nervously. "But mostly, it was him. I went into it loving sex, and met someone who loved it more. He did things to me—"

Elliot sucked air in but didn't say anything.

If he didn't like hearing that, that was his problem. He'd asked for the truth. "Ever had anyone make love to you, whisper words of love to you…in French?"

"Not really, no."

"Well, it makes you stupid."

"What happened?"

"When my trip was over, he followed me back to the States. I was dumb enough to believe it was because he was so in love with me he couldn't be without me."

"He wasn't?"

"Let's just say I underestimated the lure of a green card. We were married within months. I thought it was a whirlwind courtship. I guess, looking back, I was just being railroaded. His will is—was…stronger than mine. He mesmerized me, even though I knew he was stepping out on me almost from the start—would you believe he slept with the city hall official who married us?"

There was little he could say to that, other than, "I'm sorry."

"Even though I could see all the signs, I didn't let myself believe them. By the time I gave in and admitted the truth to myself, I already had a reason to want my marriage to work."

"Béatrice."

"Yes. But it was pretty much over. I didn't even get one free, clear year of happiness."

"Want me to find him and kick his ass?"

He was grinning like a teenager, so she was at least fifty percent sure he wasn't serious. She laughed. "You could hold him down while *I* kick his ass…" He was trying to make her feel better. It did little to erase the bitterness, but it eased the tension between them. The last thing she needed was another ugly breach with a man. She sighed. "I guess that'll teach me."

"Teach you what?"

"To buy into the picture-postcard, Caribbean-romance fantasy." She frowned, deep in her thoughts. "To buy into *any* fantasy, for that matter."

"Fantasies like…?"

"Love." The word in her mouth made her tongue feel thick, coated with a film she couldn't spit out.

His thick eyebrows lifted. "You saying you don't believe in love anymore?"

"Of course I do. I love my daughter. I value her more than my own soul."

"That's not what I meant."

"I know what you meant. I just don't have the energy to dig deep enough for an answer." Shani rubbed the side of her face contemplatively. She suddenly felt tired, a combination of three restless nights at the hospital, the vigorous, sweaty sex with Elliot and the emotional fallout she was dealing with. She wished he'd leave her alone so she could get some sleep. What was the most graceful way to throw a man out after you'd had sex?

Elliot wasn't stupid. "Finish this, honey, then I'll let you get some rest."

Sounded like a good deal to her, except she didn't know what more he wanted to hear. "I think I'm about finished, actually."

He wasn't. "Okay. If you don't want to talk anymore, that's fine. But I want to tell you something—no matter how much your husband hurt you, don't let him steal your faith. Love is always out there. You're just hurting too much to believe that."

She snorted. "If you can believe that, you've never really been hurt."

Clouds gathered in his face. "I've been hurt…."

"And yet you believe. Well, hey, if it works for you… And why wouldn't it? You live a charmed life, everything at your fingertips. Life just gives it up at your command. But we come from different worlds. You don't know me, you don't know anything about my life…"

"I want to know more—"

She went on, barely hearing him. "Just because we got into bed, and you knew which buttons to press—" oh, and the buttons he'd pressed "—doesn't mean you have a right to make pronouncements about my life. You don't know me any better now than you did an hour ago, Elliot!"

It was a low blow, and it hit its target. Before she could realize what was happening, she was being carried back into her bedroom. Not whisked lovingly in his arms like a bride on her honeymoon, but lugged over like a sack of corn and thrown onto the bed. She bounced once on the springy mattress, banging her funny bone on the bed head. "Yeeow! Careful! What're you…"

The determination on his face made her question moot. Half-dressed he might have been, but she was still completely naked, every inch of her vulnerable. As it turned out, there were only two or three square inches of her that commanded his attention. With one hand flat on the curve of her belly, he held her fast. With the other, he parted her thighs, and then he slipped his hand under her bottom to bring her to his mouth.

The first contact made her go bolt-rigid. He'd used his mouth on her earlier; teasingly, coaxingly, a prelude to more. This time he had a point to prove, and he set about it like a boxer determined to send his opponent to the mat in three rounds or less.

Really? Not likely; she'd show him otherwise. "If you think this is going to—"

He lifted his head only long enough to say, "Shut up."

He was locked in on the target and the pleasure was hard, sharp and excruciating. He kneaded her bottom, punishing her with his nails, pinching so hard she knew there'd be welts later. It didn't take long; the tigress within her wrenched itself free from its chains and went on a rampage, savaging her with bolt after bolt of pleasure.

One orgasm hit her, and then another, before she could recover from the first. As she screwed her eyes shut, she could see them, like cresting waves stacked up on a storm-tossed beach, waiting their turn. She'd denied them for so long, but now she wanted them all, even if it killed her.

His voice was muffled. He was panting. "Tell me to stop. I dare you."

Even if she was crazy enough to call a halt to this, she wouldn't be able to get a word past her dry lips. All she could do was lock her thighs around his ears, wrap her legs around his neck and clench her muscles so he couldn't break free. If he suffocated down there, too bad.

Breaking free was the last thing on his mind. As each wave slammed into shore, it sucked away a layer of sand, a layer of resistance. He didn't stop until she was too exhausted to cry out again, too swollen and sore to endure another swipe of his tongue. Her quivering thighs fell away from his ears, and a raw, harsh rasp from deep in her throat was her signal of surrender.

He knelt between her legs, looking down at her, triumphant. She waited, arms splayed, for him to fall into them. She needed his embrace. "Elliot…" Her voice sounded strange to her ears.

He stepped off the bed, a little unsteady on his feet, and stood above her as he put his shirt on. His expression was a combination of many things, only a few of them identifiable. "Guess I know enough about you to take you where I did, huh?"

Point made, Shani thought. Point definitely made. "I'm sorry."

He was done with his buttons. He rested one knee on the edge of the bed and leaned close to whisper in her ear. "And let's get one thing clear. The next time we do this—" The tinny ring of her cell phone, out in the living room where she'd tossed her bag, interrupted him.

Of one accord, they looked in its direction, but she made no move to get up. When it stopped ringing, he went on. "The next time I take you to bed," he said as a sensual smile of promise played about his lips, making anticipation leap inside her, "and it'll be *very* soon, I want you all to myself. I don't want you thinking about your ex-husband. I don't want this Christian even—"

"Christ*ophe*," she corrected.

"I don't give a crap what his name is. I don't want the jerk in bed with us. Is that clear?"

She nodded soberly, not sure whether she could fulfill his instruction, but knowing she'd be foolish to contradict him.

He looked satisfied. "Good. Because when I'm with my woman, I want her all to myself."

His woman? Before she could allow her mind to be boggled by the claim he'd staked on her, her house phone rang. The irritating jangle made it impossible to continue.

"Better get that," he suggested.

As she reached above her head, picking up the bedside extension, Elliot stepped back a few respectful paces.

"Hello?"

"You got some nerve, you know that?"

It took her sex-muddled brain several seconds to identify the voice. Yvan the Terrible. He was calling her at home? Why? "What'd you say?"

"You go and sic Elliot Bookman on me? To try to get your job back?"

Shani was stunned. Elliot had tried to get her job back?

Yvan went on. "Listen, Shani, I legitimately fired you. Matter of fact, if I recall correctly, you walked out on me—"

"My daughter was sick—"

"—and you bit a client!"

She frowned at Elliot, who wasn't exactly eavesdropping but wasn't pretending to be uninterested, either. "Could you give me a second?"

"No, *you* give *me* a second. I'm a busy man—"

She pressed the phone into her breast. "Elliot, did you ask Yvan to give me back my—"

"You're there with him?" Yvan squawked. "Shoulda known. Guy's got a way with the chicks, I'll give him that."

"That him?" Elliot asked.

She spoke into the phone. "Yes, I'm with him. But it's not what you think." Why was she explaining herself to this odious man? "Besides, what business is it of—"

Elliot began to answer, "I didn't ask him. That was—"

Yvan's harsh, nasal voice drew her attention away from Elliot. "What, you slip him some to get him to change his mind about you?"

"Did I slip him—!" She glanced at Elliot again, hoping he couldn't hear this. Given what they'd just done together, Yvan's suggestion made her feel dirty.

"Because last I saw you two together, he wasn't liking you a whole lot."

What was Yvan talking about? During the debacle in the kitchen with Stack, Elliot had been on *her* side.

"Think you can shake it like a Polaroid for a rich man and get him to call me up and threaten me, threaten *me*, to stop giving me his business, and I'll cave in? Hell no!"

She protested, outraged. "Yvan, I did not—" Then she stopped, thinking fast. Rich man? Threatening to withdraw his business? That didn't sound like Elliot. That sounded like Elliot Bookman Sr. Mystery solved.

Yvan was still shrilling at her. "Well, just so's you know, Elliot Bookman can keep his business. Think losing two or three little cocktail jobs a year's gonna make a dent in my profits? Oh no, sugarcakes. There's lots of people out there who want Yvan. Yvan doesn't need Elliot Bookman. And he sure as hell doesn't need you. You stay fired."

The phone died in her hand. She stared at it, shocked and angry. "Did you put your father up to this?"

He didn't even try to deny it. "I told him it was the fair thing to do."

"I didn't need you to do that!" Stack had been insulting and overbearing. He was the last person she needed speaking on her behalf.

"I did it anyway."

"Why?"

He looked at her for a long time, as if weighing his options between a long answer and a short. He chose the short one. He kissed her lightly on the cheek. "Stupid question." He got off the bed one last time and stood looking down at her. "You gonna be all right?"

"I'll be fine."

"Good." He checked his clothes to make sure everything

was in order. "I'll get going now. Get some rest, and I'll call you later, 'kay?"

Just the suggestion of rest made her eyelids droopy. "'Kay." He was halfway out the bedroom door when she called him back. "Elliot."

He stuck his head back in. "Hmm?"

"Wash your face before you go."

He grinned, and headed for the bathroom.

Chapter 9

Shani's autumn tomato crop was bumper this year. She loved gardening. The feel of the dirt under her fingers and the smell of it in the air connected her with nature and improved her mood. It hardly mattered that her garden was just rows of mismatched pots out on her back porch.

She carefully set her vine-ripened tomatoes into the basket and put down her garden clippers. She was in the mood for homemade Bolognese. When Bee came home from day care later, she'd be in her glee.

"You know you're gonna fall, right?"

Bee's new kitten, a female with black and white markings that reminded Shani of a cow, balanced on the porch railing, its blue-green eyes conveying exactly how laughable it found Shani's concern. Her? Fall? Get real.

"Well, don't say I didn't warn you," she clucked. She watched as the creature, such a tiny repository for so much arrogance, made its way along the railing, delicately setting one paw in front the next, like a ballerina practicing at the barre. As much as she didn't want to admit it, Elliot's ill-advised but well-meaning gift to her daughter had brought a spark of joy into her life, too. Puddin', as Bee had jubilantly named her, was constantly underfoot, didn't necessarily use the litter box *all* the time and had taken to sleeping on Shani's pillow, usually with the tip of her tail wrapped around Shani's neck like a fox stole. But Puddin' was also good company, and in the past few weeks, Shani had grown grateful for that.

The buzzer at her front door went off. Puddin's ears pricked up. So did Shani's. She checked her watch. Was it noon already? She'd been so engrossed in her gardening she'd let time slip past. Elliot was here. With his tech company on flexitime and employees setting their own schedules, he was usually able to get away when he wanted. Most days, he spent a fervent hour in her bed, and then, when she was satiated and glowing, they shared a lazy lunch on the couch, listening to music and talking.

Today, though, they were going out to lunch, a little Italian ristorante with a view of De Menzes Park. It would be nice to go out for a change. Her only contact with the outside world was the seven-block stroll to Bee's day care and the occasional visit to the grocery store, so she was going stir-crazy.

She patted herself down in panic. There was enough dirt under her nails to grow radishes, she didn't have on a smidge of makeup and her hair was mussed. She laughed to herself at the last part. He'd seen her often enough with her hair mussed, but usually it was he who did the mussing.

The buzzer went again. "Coming!" She picked up her basket, with its tomatoes nestled among the bell peppers and clippings of basil, parsley and chives, and hurried inside. Puddin' was right behind—well, not just behind, but between. Ankles, that is. Shani yanked open the door, not bothering to set her basket down first, an expectant smile on her face.

Stack Bookman was standing there. He was wearing a neutral, pin-striped suit of the deepest charcoal, with a surprising pale orange shirt and a skinny, deep orange tie of rich paisley brocade. You could have measured the dimple under the knot with a precision instrument and found it to be dead center. He held a slim alligator briefcase casually at his side; it glowed as if it had been hand-buffed.

Dashing he might be, but he wasn't exactly a friend, yet he was standing on her doorstep, looking as if he expected her to let him in. "What're you doing here?"

The thick brows, so much like Elliot's, didn't even lift at her tone. "I needed to speak to you."

Speak to her? This was the man who'd pawed her and tried to convince her she should be grateful for his attention, seeing how much he liked dark women and all. She shouldn't let it rankle, but "shouldn't" and "didn't" were two different things. "Appears to me you said enough the last time."

His dark umber eyes seemed to hold genuine regret. "Mrs. Matthieu, I'm very sorry about what happened that night. I had a little too much to drink." He gave a soft, dismissive laugh. "I know that's not an excuse—"

"Damned Skippy, it's not." She transferred the basket to the other hand, pressing it against her hip.

Stack looked down at the kitten at her feet. Puddin' was eyeballing her visitor as if she was wondering if he was good to eat. Stack's Adam's apple leaped.

"She bothering you?" Shani asked.

After a few seconds' delay, he forced his lips into a curve. "Not a fan of cats, actually."

Shani shrugged. One more difference between father

and son. Elliot lavished his attention on the little fuzzball. Almost made her wonder if he liked cats more because his father didn't.

Stack's eyes were steady on hers again. "I'm here to try to make it up to you."

He had to be kidding. She stepped away to put the basket down, trusting that Puddin's unwavering presence in the doorway would act as a deterrent. Which would have made her laugh, if she wasn't so irritated. An eighteen-ounce bit of fluff was standing in her doorway like a protective pot hound—and keeping her unwelcome visitor at bay. She turned back to him. "I don't think that's possible, Mr. Bookman. If you've come to apologize, great. Let's just say for argument's sake you've done so. Now, please…"

"I needed to apologize, yes, but there's more to it than that…."

She tried not to look at her watch again. If Elliot turned up now and found his father here….

"Please," he went on, "I'd prefer to discuss this inside."

She crossed her arms, wishing she still had the garden shears in her grip. Sharp metal had a way of giving a girl confidence. She examined him critically. Tall, fit, urbane, he was nothing like the Stack who'd groped her in the kitchen. He was clear-eyed, sober and humble. Maybe it was the humility that got to her. She stifled her misgivings and stood aside.

He gave her a grateful nod, but didn't move. "If you don't mind…" He pointed with his chin at the kitten sitting across her threshold like a lion at Trafalgar Square.

She suppressed a grin. Stack Bookman: powerful, wealthy, conceited…and afraid of cats. She scooped Puddin' up, tucked her under her arm and led the way. Stack followed, taking care to lock the door behind him, as if being in her little run-down neighborhood made him nervous.

He sat without being invited in the large overstuffed love seat. "May I have a glass of water?"

She suspected he was hankering for something harder than water, but she left quickly and returned just as quickly with a glass filled from the tap. She handed it over with as much grace as she could muster. He drank half of it in one draught, and then began looking around. She gave him a few moments to take everything in: the little kiddie tent pitched against a wall, where Bee crawled in to play with her toys, the warm orange of the rug, the photos and prints. He scrutinized the photo of the fishing boats on the beach that Christophe had given her. "The islands?"

She nodded.

"South Sea?"

"Martinique, actually."

He dragged his eyes away, back to her. "Been there?"

"It's where I met my husband. He took that picture." She wasn't in the mood to indulge in small talk, though. "Maybe you should get to the—"

"Point. Right." He cleared his throat. "Yvan didn't rehire you."

If she was looking for a trigger, that was it. "I don't need for you to go behind my back and try to get me back my job. I can get a job on my own, thank you—"

"Have you?"

Shani thought of Bee's unpaid hospital bill and the first alimony check that was due but which—unsurprisingly—hadn't arrived yet. She shook her head. "I've got some applications out, but no responses yet. I still don't need—"

"My son tells me you're a single mom. I know it's hard to take care of a child these days…."

Shani tensed, enough for Puddin', still nestled in her arms, to react to the sudden rigidity in her muscles by digging in with her tiny cactus-needle claws. "Elliot's been talking to you? About me?"

"No, no, not like that. Elliot's a very private person. And besides…" He looked both regretful and sheepish…. "We don't have a whole lot to say to each other, most of the time."

"I noticed." Which didn't answer the question. She watched him, frowning.

"Sit down, will you?"

She surprised herself by obeying an order to sit in her own chair. She guessed Stack was used to issuing commands that weren't often breached. She perched on the edge of the armchair, holding the kitten in her lap like an armored girdle.

"The thing is, Mrs….look, can I call you Shani?"

She shrugged. "I don't see why not."

"The thing is, Shani…I'm here to try to make things right. I have investments in a lot of businesses, most of them here in Santa Amata. Real estate, manufacturing, publishing…"

"I know."

"I've got half interest in a publisher that produces academic texts…" He paused. Waiting for her to get where he was coming from.

She didn't. "What about it?"

"We're working on a series of history texts for high school. Three books on postslavery black history, throughout North and South America and the Caribbean. I was thinking you could help with that."

He wasn't suggesting… "Help…how?"

"You could be an academic consultant of sorts. My writers have completed a draft of the first book. You could edit the copy for content and accuracy. Help ensure they're in line with the school curriculum."

"I'm a waitress," she stuttered. "What do I know about…?"

"We both know you're more than a waitress."

Shani had the odd, panicked sensation of drowning without water. Stack Bookman knew. If he knew she was a history professor, then he knew how she'd lost her job. She felt queasy, hot with embarrassment. "How'd you know that?"

"Someone at the party recognized you. A businessman, visiting from France. He told me about your…uh… situation."

Stack knew what she'd done, or, rather, what her husband had done to her. "And have you…seen them? The photographs, I mean?"

Although he didn't hedge, he was discreet. "My colleague had a copy of the magazine couriered over to me once he got back to the Cote d'Azur."

"Why?"

He was gracious enough to look ashamed. "I'd asked him to, at the party. At the time I thought it was, well, amusing."

Amusing. Shani wished she was wearing a nun's habit, sackcloth, anything other than the white fitted jeans and thin, clingy old hoodie with the broken zipper and nothing under it. The man perched on her love seat, holding her in his unwavering stare, had seen her naked.

She clamped her knees together. That sudden, impulsive movement was more than Puddin' could bear. With a yowl of indignation, the kitten popped off her thighs, crossed the space between Shani and Stack in a single pounce, and bounded across Stack's lap—making him blanch—before disappearing into Bee's little tent.

Anger gave her embarrassment a sharper edge. "Did he tell you this before or after you molested me in the kitchen?"

He didn't even challenge the accusation of molestation. "Some time before that."

"Was that what made you think I'd be easy?"

He shook his head. "What I did was a reflection on my character, not yours. But I've apologized for that, and I don't want to go over it again. I lost you your job, and I'm here to make amends. I'm here to offer you work."

Work? How could she work for him when... "You've seen me naked."

"Not in person."

That made it *so* much better! "Photos are bad enough. And these didn't leave anything to the imagination, did they."

He didn't even blink. "No, they didn't. But I'm not proposing to hire you as a nude model. I'm asking for your expertise as an authority on black history."

"I don't know if I can."

"You know the material. You know how these kids think, how they talk. I don't want some dry old boring book they're never going to open. I want something hip, or whatever word they're using these days that I'm too old to know about." He gave a practiced laugh.

He pressed on with the assurance of a seasoned businessman who knew he was about to clinch a deal. "Don't even think of denying your abilities. I've got a list of the papers you've published, the books you've consulted on, right here in my briefcase. You want me to slap a copy of your own bibliography down in front of you?"

"I know what I've written."

"Good. So we're not going the route of denial, hmm?"

There was a whole lot she wished she could deny, but

her abilities weren't among them. She sniffed. There was more in the air than Stack's cologne. It was the sweet scent of temptation—intellectual temptation, at least. History was her passion; black history in the Americas, her pet topic. Offering her the opportunity to get her hands on three fresh, new, unpublished books on the subject was like hiring a paint huffer to work security detail in a hardware store.

But she'd been tottering around in a silly waitress outfit and slinging hors d'oeuvres for such a long time... She hedged. "I haven't taught in a while."

"This isn't about teaching—"

"I know, but, I'm a little rusty."

"That's crap, and you know it. The knowledge is always there." He gestured in the direction of her wicker bookshelf, which was groaning under the weight of her books. "I don't need to walk over there to know what those books are about. You still read, don't you?"

"When my daughter gives me a free moment..."

"Exactly who this is about. Your daughter." He knew she was wavering, and he pushed gently to topple her over. "Think about her. The pay's competitive. You've been out of work for a couple of weeks now, not so? I'm sure those bills must be adding up."

She looked around the living room, her thoughts racing faster than her gaze. The inhabitants of the Hundred Acre Wood flopped about on the floor: Tigger and Pooh, Piglet and Eeyore. There were more bees than she could count, stuffed ones, wooden ones, plastic ones, broken and whole. Bee. Her medication had rivaled this month's grocery bill, and as for the hospital bill, it would make a dent the size of a Buick in her savings fund. Whether Christophe was going to stick to the agreement of the divorce and send her an alimony check was still up in the air. She wasn't banking on it—pardon the pun. He hadn't been all that meticulous about paying child support before, either.

Stack sensed her hesitation, and like all good predators, he pounced. He clicked open his briefcase, pulled out a slip of paper and held it out. "While you're thinking about it, have a look at my offer. See if it helps you make up your mind."

She held it gingerly by the corner and scanned it. Damn him; the money was good. But to work for Stack, a man who'd made lascivious suggestions and pawed her breast? A man who'd seen her butt-naked, in full color, in a series of poses that went beyond suggestive? Good grief, no.

"You can do most of your work from home. You only have to go into the office once or twice a week to consult with the authors and the senior editor." As if able to read her thoughts, he added with a wry smile. "You don't even have to see me."

The numbers on the bottom line bounced up and down like Mexican jumping beans. She did a quick calculation. Bee's hospital bill: gone. *And* there'd be enough left to keep her scintillating lifestyle going for another few months. But how would Elliot react?

Elliot; God, he'd be here any minute now. If this needed to be done, it needed to be done pronto. Stack had to be in his car and away from here in…she glanced surreptitiously at her watch…negative time. She pinched the bridge of her nose and nodded. "Do I need to sign this?"

"It's not a contract. I'll have one done and delivered by the end of the week." Stack rose, pleased. His handshake was firm, warm and brief; a gentleman's handshake.

"Thank you, Stack."

He inclined his head. The curves at the corners of his mouth made no secret of his triumph. "Thank *you*, for the opportunity to redeem myself. And for your help. I know you'll do a great job."

Now that the dreaded man-eating kitten was no longer a threat, Stack's stride to the door was more confident. He allowed her to unlock it for him and stepped out onto the landing. He paused, regarding her soberly.

Which was just as well, because she had something to say. But how to begin? "Stack?"

She could tell he knew what was coming. "Yes?"

"About the photographs…"

He was surprisingly kind. "I take it my son doesn't know about them?"

She grimaced and shook her head. "No, and I'd rather…"

"I'm good at keeping secrets," he assured her, and left without saying anything more.

She leaned over the railing and looked down into the street, following his confident gait along the sidewalk until he slid into the Lexus. It glided away from the curb as if it was supported by a current of warm air.

A chill easily penetrated her hoodie, making the hair along her arms stand up. A job. Not a full-on nine-to-five, but a job nonetheless. Her money problems were solved in the short term; there'd be time for her to decide what she'd do next. To figure out if she had the courage to face a lecture hall again. That was a relief. But her relief was tainted by a vague queasy sensation. She hoped it was just hunger.

Chapter 10

"Tell me you didn't!" Elliot looked at Shani in disbelief. The afternoon wasn't going as he'd planned. He'd pulled up to her apartment, a few minutes late, eager to take Shani out for a change. For the past few weeks, he'd been a pig, dragging her off to the bedroom every time he visited. He told himself he couldn't help it; it was the first time he'd met someone as greedily sexual as he was.

But she was a lady, all the same, and a lady needed to be taken out and dined, not kept hidden away in an apartment like a secret mistress. So he'd cleaned up nice, even going as far as to get his hair cut—never mind he'd miss the sensation of Shani pulling on it—and arrived expecting her to be prettied up and waiting. Instead he found her pacing outside the restaurant downstairs, dressed in the world's rattiest hoodie, and insisting they take a walk around the neighborhood...because they needed to talk.

We need to talk. The four words in the English language

guaranteed to cause a man's guts—and various body parts slightly south of them—to shrivel with dread. Naturally, the first thing to come to his mind—the first thing to come to any man's mind—was an image of layettes and lullabies, even though he was always meticulously careful when it came to matters of protection and contraception. She'd started walking without his yea or nay, so he'd had little choice but to catch up to her. His mind had wildly flailed about, trying to bring his terror under control, while she'd walked in silence for a full five minutes, until she put an end to his diaper-scented fears—but dropped a bombshell of a different sort.

"I don't have a choice. I have bills to pay. I have a daughter to raise." She puffed, small tendrils of warm air curling from between her lips. She pumped her arms as she walked, elbows out, a barrier against him as they headed east on Bagley, in the direction of Independence Avenue.

"But of all the people you could choose to work for… Couldn't you get something else?"

"I've tried. The market's tight. This'll keep me until I find something permanent."

"But my dad's—"

"A legitimate businessman. It's a great offer." She sounded as if she was trying to convince herself as much as him.

"But editing history books? I don't understand…" Shouldn't she be job hunting in restaurants? He felt as if he had most of the pieces of a puzzle but not the box they came in. The whole picture was escaping him.

She gave him a maddeningly evasive look. "Guess you could say waitressing wasn't my first calling."

Guess you could say that. "What was?"

They stepped aside to avoid colliding with a dozen preschoolers tramping one behind the next, looking like a fuzzy, multicolored caterpillar. "I used to be a professor of black history over at State." She said it as if she was announcing she'd been an undercover agent for the KGB.

He absorbed this information slowly. "Okay." He remembered the books crammed into her bookcase. African religion and art. New World history. Battle and conquest in the Caribbean. He'd never done much more than idly run a finger along their spines. He could kick himself. Maybe if he'd been more observant, they'd have prodded him into asking a question. Avoided getting whacked between the eyes by this information now. Questions like: "So how's a college professor become a waitress?"

She hedged. "It's a long story."

"I've got time, babe." He saw her shiver, even though at the pace she was going, she should have been working up quite a sweat. He considered suggesting they turn tail and get the hell back to her place, but he was afraid to break the momentum of their conversation. Instead, he dragged off his suede jacket and placed it around her shoulders.

She pushed her arms in, neglecting to zip it up, but didn't acknowledge the gesture otherwise. "I used to teach college history, before I met Christophe. I met him while I was doing research for a paper, I told you…"

Right. She'd let that little gem slip around the time she was regaling him with details of how good her ex was in bed. "French-Caribbean slavery, I remember. Runaway slaves."

"The *nègres marrons,* yes. He was helping me with that when we…" She glanced up at him through the hair flopping over her face and wisely kept on track. "Um, anyhow…" She blinked, the kind of blink a poker player gives when she's about to bluff her way through a hand. "It didn't work out."

He knew he wasn't getting the whole truth, and that made him want to scream. "What's that even mean?"

"It means by that time my marriage was unraveling. I filed for divorce, my husband moved out. The teaching job…fell apart. That's all I can tell you."

He frowned, trying to search her face even though he was seeing it in profile. What was he seeing? Guilt? Shame? Knowing she wasn't telling him everything made him want to kick one of the huge oaks lining the street. He'd probably crack a toe, but the physical pain would distract him from the ache of knowing she didn't trust him enough to spill whatever she was bottling up.

He had a passing urge to make a few calls to the university, see what he could find out, but he shoved the idea to the back of his mind. Sneakiness just wasn't in his character. He'd have to persuade her to tell him of her own free will. But how? "It just 'fell apart'?"

Her jaw worked behind those pretty lips. "Sometimes jobs do that, Elliot. Whole careers can fall apart. Not that *you'd* know."

Yeow. He touched his cheek, expecting to find scratches from her claws. "Come again?"

"Your business is so successful, half the time, you don't even have to be there. You drive around in your damn pink sports car—" she waved at the busy street "—that probably costs more than my apartment." She tugged at the lapel of the jacket she had draped around herself. "What you paid for this jacket would feed us for a month. You've got nothing to worry about. How can I expect you to understand what I'm going through?"

He stopped abruptly, feet crunching in the fall leaves,

forcing her to stop, too. They were near the entrance to a music store that was shrilling out some trash metal CD—wasn't trash metal dead?—loud enough to seriously get on his nerves. But not as much as Shani's contemptuous dismissal of him did. He brought his face close to hers, words cracking. "My business is successful because I put everything I have into it. My time, my energy, my skills and my knowledge. I also happen to be in a market that's growing, but don't hate me because I made the right choices. And furthermore—" the pounding bass from the CD-store speakers penetrated to his bones "—don't judge me because I leave my business in the hands of others for a few hours, just so I can spend time with *you*."

Her mouth puckered as if she'd sucked on a sour lemon. "I'm sorry, Elliot."

Sorry wasn't what he wanted. What he wanted was for her to give up this stupid idea of working for Stack. An idea flashed, relationship kryptonite, but desperate times called for desperate measures. "Come work for me."

She was aghast. *"What?"*

"Let me give you a job."

"As what?"

He threw up his hands. "I don't know. I can figure something out…."

She sputtered. "Just what I need to be. The boss's bimbo."

"That's not what—"

"You run a tech company. You can read code like other people read English! What the hell do I know about that?"

"You don't have to. We can find something. Anything, just so you don't have to go work for *him*!"

Then she asked the question he'd hoped they'd never have to deal with. "Why do you hate your father so much?"

His answer bulleted out of him before he could hold it back. "Other than the fact that he killed my mother?"

Shani blanched. "Stack murdered your mom?"

He wished he could say yes and leave it at that; maybe it'd scare her out of taking this stupid job. He should be ashamed for wanting that, given how badly she needed the money, but everybody needed to be selfish once in a while. Honesty forced him to clarify: "He didn't drown her in the tub or poison her coffee, if that's what you're thinking."

"Then how...?"

He thought of the beautiful, gentle soul that had been Janice Bookman. The talented, graceful, smart woman his father hadn't deserved—and who hadn't deserved Stack's endless, careless infidelities. "He made her life miserable. As a child, I remember my mother crying the nights he didn't come home. I remember the arguments." His lips twisted with the memory.

Pain stopped him. It was like opening shoe boxes filled with mementos that had been shoved under his bed and half forgotten. Why was he sharing them with Shani? "When I was fourteen, I found out he was sleeping with my aunt—"

"Your mom's sister?"

"Right. I went over to his office one afternoon and told him he'd better cut that crap out. He told me to mind my own business. Said when I was a man, I'd understand. So I decked him."

"Did he hit you back?"

"No. Don't understand why, though. He'd have been justified. It hasn't exactly been man hugs between us since."

"But you talk to him. You were at his party…"

He shrugged. "He's my father."

"And what about…your mom?" She phrased the question delicately, as if she knew how much it would hurt for him to answer it. He almost loved her for that. But that clanging and banging in his head…that music! "Can we get away from this noise?"

Her head snapped in the direction of the storefront speakers, as if she hadn't even noticed the music before. "Yeah, sure. We could move up a ways, find a place to sit."

He grabbed her by the elbow and they walked a few yards. They were well within sight of Independence Avenue, the busy artery that intersected downtown Santa Amata. The noise being vomited out of the speakers gave way to the vroom of traffic. He looked around. "We should sit—if we could find a bench."

"No matter."

"I've got to get you a seat."

"No matter, Elliot. C'mere." She marched up to the neon yellow front wall of a small design studio and plopped herself down on the sidewalk, leaning backward and yanking him down next to her. She let her hands flop onto her knees. "Tell me."

Her eyes were on him, her mouth slightly open, as if she didn't want to let a word slip past her, so he let the whole ugly story spew. "'Bout a year after that fight between me and Stack, she had an affair of her own. Some guy in her office. She and my father owned a real estate company. My mother managed it. She was miserable. She fell for this guy and they started a thing. Can't say I blamed her."

"And your father…"

"Went ballistic. I heard them in their bedroom,

screaming at each other. He called her a slut, told her she should be ashamed of herself. In those days, Stack wasn't drinking as much as now, but I guess he'd stopped to have a few on his way home that day."

"He was mad at her for doing the same thing he was doing all along?"

"My thoughts exactly. She even said as much. He told her that was different. He was a man—that was his option. She was a woman—it was her job to stick by her man and take care of her kid. He told her if she didn't break it off he was going to divorce her, force her out of the company and sue for custody of me."

"He wanted you?"

Elliot laughed bitterly. "He barely spoke to me. It was just good leverage." He shrugged. "Probably wouldn't have got away with it. I was old enough to speak my mind to a judge, if it came to that. But it scared her badly enough to end things with this guy. Then, going to the office and seeing him every day got too hard, so she stopped working. She didn't even have her family's support. They blamed her for the affair her sister had with Stack. They said if she was taking care of business with their sex life, it would never have happened."

"I'm really sorry, Elliot." She tried to touch his arm.

"Cut that out." He pulled away, wishing he didn't see the pity in her eyes. It was worse than having her all bristle-haired and mad at him. He delivered the coup de grâce bluntly, almost belligerently. "A few months later she drove her car off Falcon River Bridge. Cops ruled it an accident, but I know it was suicide."

"How could you know that?"

"She called me from the car. She said she just wanted to hear my voice. She was crying. Nothing's ever scared me that much. The phone went dead, and I knew. I didn't know how she was going to do it, or where, but I knew. I called my father. He told me I was worrying over nothing."

Elliot shook his head, his mind slipping back into the past. He remembered running out of the house, into the street, heading the way his mother usually came. Running for miles and keeping on even when his lungs were tearing. Wanting to look for her, but not sure where to start. There was a crowd at Falcon River Bridge. Cop cars and fire engines. He knew in his heart that she was down there, swallowed up by the black water.

He'd told them about the call, of course, but Stack, with his gift for making people see only what he wanted them to, had managed to discredit him, saying he was distraught, closing the door on any suicide investigation. His mother's insurance policy benefited Elliot. His father's reputation as a grieving widower brought women to him in droves. Everybody won.

He was grateful when Shani ignored his instruction to leave him alone. She reached out and cradled his head, pulling it down. He loved the way her breasts felt against his cheek. But even so, the resurrected, reheated pain made him add harshly: "That's the man you want to work for."

She released him jerkily. "You aren't being fair. It's a good job, and I need work. Besides, most of it will mean working from home. I don't have to see him if I don't want to."

"Oh, you'll see him. He'll make sure of it." He knew he was being petulant, whining like a kid, but every time he thought about his mother, he was instantly transformed into the teenager she'd left behind. Still needing her mothering. Desperately wanting Shani to make this sacrifice, as a show of loyalty.

"Like I told you," she answered, "sometimes life means making hard choices. Even if you don't know what that feels like, understand that some people do." She got to her feet abruptly and dusted off the seat of her white pants, which weren't all that white anymore.

He followed suit, defeated.

She tried to smile. "You were taking me for lunch. We could head back to the apartment, and if you give me ten, I can spruce up a little." Her voice had the forced cheeriness people used to jolly people who didn't want to be jollied. "I could go for something hot and spicy right now."

"I don't feel very hungry."

"Well, then let's…" She paused, looking unsure of how to voice what she was suggesting. Then she let her lips explain silently. Her kiss was different. Not passionate and daring and hungry. It was soft, tender, consoling. Pitying. He responded in spite of himself, kissing her eagerly back, but forced himself to stop. She was trying to make him feel better, that much was evident. But did she really think a little sex would be all it took?

She smiled, already half turning in the direction they'd come from. "No sense freezing out here. We could stay in, and I could make you forget…for a little while."

Just what he needed; a doggie treat. "I don't need you to make me forget. Sex isn't a consolation prize."

Her face was the picture of puzzled hurt. "Consolation prize? I was trying to make love to you!"

"Not today, Shani." He dragged himself out of her field of influence. Better to get away from her fast, before he gave in to his screaming body and did what it wanted him to do. *You crazy, man?* his erection protested. "Can you make it back to your place okay?"

"I live here," she reminded him.

"Then I think I'll keep on walking awhile." He took several paces and turned back to see her still standing in the same spot. "I'm not mad at you," he comforted.

"Hmm."

"I'll call you later."

She lifted her shoulders, still wearing his jacket, and let them fall again. They eyed each other, an unspoken challenge between them to see who would turn away first.

He did.

Chapter 11

Shani held the thick, flat package in her hand. It was wrapped in brown paper and tied with string. She stroked the paper covering with her fingertips, enjoying the waxy feel. It contained the final manuscript of the first textbook, which for some reason, Stack had asked her to deliver to him, in person.

Odd, considering the hands-off stance he'd taken with the project, but he probably wanted to be around when the baby was delivered, so to speak. So she'd walked with a show of confidence into his office building, her demure yellow wool dress and low pumps providing a feminine kind of body armor against the nervousness she still battled in his presence. She never forgot the fact that this man had seen her resplendently naked in full, glossy color. It was enough to make any woman nervous.

"Mrs. Matthieu..." Stack's secretary wasn't what Shani would have expected in an employee of his: a severe-looking older woman in a tailored suit, rather than a lip-glossed bleached blonde in a short skirt. "Mr. Bookman will see you now."

Shani took a cleansing breath, trying to draw in the soothing scents of mandarin and lavender from Stack's aromatherapy diffusers. It was Elliot's thirtieth birthday, and she'd asked him out, wanting to spend some of the money she was earning on him for a change. She planned a sweet, romantic dinner, with a special treat afterward. She'd have just enough time to get this meeting over with, and hurry home to make herself gorgeous.

She stepped across the threshold and half turned to thank the woman, but she had already shut the door, leaving her alone and staring across a wide expanse of gray-flecked carpet. Stack's desk was the size of a life raft and as clean as a surgical table, save for a pen holder, a phone and his folded hands.

"Shani!" His smile was one of pleasant surprise, almost as if he hadn't been the one to ask her here.

She held up her paper-wrapped manuscript as if it were a riot officer's shield. "Hi."

"Come on in. No...don't sit there. My desk...it's the size of a damn Ping-Pong table." He waved her in the direction of a little alcove. It held two buff-colored leather armchairs, a couch, a coffee table and a minibar. "Sit yourself down."

She followed him, wishing she could toss the package onto the table and run. Consciously or otherwise, she chose the armchair closest to the door.

He gave her a discerning look. "You all right?"

"Fine." Damned if she would let him know he still made her nervous. She wished she'd brought her kitten to back her up.

Stack went over to the bar and picked up two glasses. "Maybe a drink?"

"No, thank you."

"Aw, come on. It'll make you feel better."

"Well…" To be honest, her throat had clamped down on itself. "Soda, then."

"Anything in that soda?" His eyes, so much like Elliot's, held the same mischievous glitter.

"I'd rather not."

"Suit yourself. Mind if I do?"

She made a *go-ahead* gesture.

He poured himself a few generous fingers of gin, added a drop of tonic, then got her an orange juice with a dash of bitters and fizzed it up with the rest of his tonic. He held it out. "Ladies like this."

She was sure they did. It tasted like a mimosa without the sting. She set the package down between them and they sipped their drinks quietly. She considered pretending she wasn't interested in the things such an urbane, wealthy and self-indulgent man would surround himself with, but she decided the heck with it and gazed frankly around.

The color of the walls made her think of a forest of bamboo. Pity they were adorned with three awful paintings, which looked as if they'd been done by a herd of elephants hopped up on fermented sugar cane.

"Hideous, huh?"

She dragged her eyes away from the spectacle. "'Scuse me?"

"Butt-ugly, aren't they?" He pointed at the paintings.

She floundered for a polite response.

Stack laughed. "You don't have to lie. We're friends…."

She wouldn't go *that* far….

"And we're neither of us blind. Those paintings look like yesterday's lunch. But that's not art. That's an investment.

THE EDITOR'S "THANK YOU" FREE GIFTS INCLUDE:

Two Kimani™ Romance Novels
Two exciting surprise gifts

YES! I have placed my Editor's "thank you" Free Gifts seal in the space provided at right. Please send me 2 FREE books, and my 2 FREE Mystery Gifts. I understand that I am under no obligation to purchase anything further, as explained on the back of this card.

PLACE FREE GIFTS SEAL HERE

About how many NEW paperback fiction books have you purchased in the past 3 months?

❏ 0-2 ❏ 3-6 ❏ 7 or more

FDCD FDCP FDCZ

168/368 XDL

Please Print

FIRST NAME

LAST NAME

ADDRESS

APT.#   CITY

STATE/PROV.   ZIP/POSTAL CODE

Thank You!

BUSINESS REPLY MAIL

FIRST-CLASS MAIL   PERMIT NO. 717   BUFFALO, NY

POSTAGE WILL BE PAID BY ADDRESSEE

THE READER SERVICE

PO BOX 1867

BUFFALO NY 14240-9952

NO POSTAGE
NECESSARY
IF MAILED
IN THE
UNITED STATES

Guy who did those? He's, like, a hundred and three. When he kicks it, the value of those things is going to triple." His grin was triumphant.

With that new information at her disposal, she stared at the paintings again. It was no use. She let air whistle through her closed lips. "Nope. Still look like crap."

They both laughed, and there was silence again. Shani reached out and ran her fingers along the brown string holding her package together, like a nervous young girl twisting her engagement ring.

Stack broke the silence. "That the manuscript?"

She pushed it across the table at him. "It is."

He didn't pick it up. "Heard you did a great job."

She was pleased, but still cautious. "Thank you. It's good to be back doing what I love. Waitressing lets you meet people, but I always find dead people more interesting." She caught herself. The whole issue of being back in academia pointed to her reasons for leaving in the first place. She hoped he didn't make the connection.

No such luck. His eyes flickered over her body. Then his gaze was steady on her face again, circumspect, unwavering.

Enough, she decided. Time to take control. Crisp and businesslike, she asked, "Stack, why'd you invite me over?"

He smiled. "Enough of the small talk, eh?"

"Something like that."

"I wanted to thank you for your work."

"You could've done that over the phone."

He nodded to concede her point, and then, *whap*, right out of left field, came his question: "You and my son an item?"

She gaped. "How'd that become your business?"

He didn't look as if he thought the question was the

least bit inappropriate. "Just wondering. He's my son. I'm interested in what's taking place in his life. As it is, he doesn't share much of it with me."

Any wonder? she thought but knew better than to say.

Stack went on. "So, are you?"

The clack of her glass on the tabletop was even louder than Stack's. She shot to her feet. "I don't see the point in having this conversation." She turned to go.

He lifted a hand to stop her. "I hope I didn't offend you."

"You did."

"I'm sorry. I just want to know what's going on with my son." He smiled his hypnotic serpent's smile, baring teeth he'd spent good money on.

Her body swayed toward the door, anxious to get away, and then back to face Stack again.

"He upset that you're doing this?" he asked.

"Doing what?" Elliot didn't even know she was here. He'd have a fit.

"Doing this job for me."

She touched her tongue anxiously to her bottom lip, and that was all he needed to know. He nodded soberly. She tried to stonewall. "If you want to know how Elliot feels about anything, ask him yourself."

"Wouldn't work. You know that."

"I'm not surprised. After what happened…" She halted.

Too late. Stack's face was the picture of consternation. "He told you? About Janice…his mother?" The dense brows drew together. "He must really care for you."

"Why?"

"I don't think my son's talked to a soul about his mother in years."

Her frown matched Stack's: contemplative and surprised. What did that mean? Was the fact that Elliot had shared his pain a sign that he cared about her, or had it just been a means of thwarting his father's attempts to hire her? No, Elliot wasn't like that. He wouldn't play dirty. If Stack was right, then Elliot had allowed her to see a private part of himself that he didn't share with other women. That alone opened up a host of wonderful—and scary—possibilities.

She needed to get out so she could think. "Look, Stack. I'm grateful for the job, but you hired me to edit textbooks, not to discuss Elliot. So I think I'd better go—"

He pleaded, "Just give me five minutes."

"Why?"

"Because I want my son to be my friend again. And maybe you can help."

"How could I help? And why would I want to? The two of you have issues. It's up to you—"

"Sit, Shani. Please. Five minutes, that's all I ask. At least listen to my side of the story."

In spite of loud protests deep inside, she dropped back into the chair, sitting with her knees pressed tightly closed and her hands clasped around them like metal bands padlocked around a treasure chest. His side of the story? What other side could there be?

He hesitated. "I don't know how much he told you…"

"I think you can guess."

He sighed painfully. "I was a good husband to Janice…."

Was he serious? "You cheated on her every chance you got!"

"You women, everything in your life touches everything else. For men, it's different. We have our life with our families, our businesses and our private, separate lives."

He looked at her carefully and saw she wasn't convinced. "It's difficult for a woman to understand."

She'd heard that argument a dozen times, coming from her ex-husband, and she *still* didn't understand. "You cheated on her with her sister!"

His skin grew mottled as the blood rushed to his face. "That was a mistake."

"What about your son? What kind of example did you think you were setting for a young boy? Did you think it was right, allowing him to grow up watching you treat his mother like you did?"

Stack defended himself roughly. "My son's no slouch when it comes to womanizing, either. Let me assure you— he's no angel."

That's where he was wrong. Elliot *was* an angel, one who'd swooped in and offered her sanctuary when she most needed it. "Your son hasn't made any vows to anyone. He can take whoever he pleases to bed."

"Including you?"

"You're out of line!" The only reason she didn't get up again was that Stack had dropped to the seat beside her. He twisted to face her and she felt the light pressure of his hands on her forearms, not restraining her as much as urging her to stay put. Her body went rigid, assailed by the memory of his intrusion upon her space that night in his kitchen.

He sensed her reaction and exhaled sharply. "I'm doing this all wrong…"

"Damn right. Let me up."

"I just need your help. It's not easy for me to ask for it."

"Let me up, Stack, or I'll…" She remembered the bite she'd clamped on his hand the last time. She wasn't far from delivering a second, more ferocious dose.

"I love my son. I want to mend this thing between us. I want to know what's happening with him."

"And you want me to tell you?"

His grip on her was insistent. "Not any, uh, intimate details. Just what he's thinking, what he's feeling…" His face was close…too close. She could hear and feel him breathe.

Then, in an incredible flash of clarity, she realized to her horror he was about to kiss her. She bucked like a marlin on the deck of a fishing boat, shoving him hard with all her strength, and slipped past, running toward the door.

By the time her hand was on the doorknob, Stack was behind her. "I'm sorry."

"What the hell did you think you were doing?"

He looked as stunned as she felt. "I have no idea. I got carried away…"

"You get carried away a lot."

"You misunderstood—" He was so anxious to preserve his crumbling composure he was willing to lie.

"You're unbelievable. First you ask me to betray him, carry news for you, and then you have the gall to think I'd let you…" She fought the urge to throw up. "What made you think I'd let you touch me, when you know I'm in love—" She choked off the rest.

In love with Elliot? She put her hand to her mouth as if she could feel the heat of the revelation there. Sure, there was passion between them; affection even. Warmth… tenderness. But love? She wasn't ready for that.

Stack's eyes were as wide as hers. "In love with him?" He shook his head. "No, I didn't know that." His gaze was sharp and discerning. "Looks like you didn't, either."

She had to get out. She didn't want this man intruding on her revelation; she needed time alone to deal with the turmoil it brought and to find a solution. Because this was the last thing she needed. She'd barely had enough time to get over Christophe, and now Elliot was poised to rock her like a hurricane.

And then there was Stack. Agreeing to work for him had been a bad idea. Staying in the job would be a worse one. "You know what? I can't do this anymore. I'm done."

He was aghast. "You're quitting? But…the other books…"

"Find someone else," she said shortly, blocking out the rational voice that reminded her how much she needed the money. "Apart from the fact that you have…control issues…spying on Elliot's not part of my job description." She shook her head ruefully. "I'm not—"

There was a buzzing, insistent and loud. Her cell phone. She fished it from her purse and looked at the number. The area code was Martinique's.

Her stomach dropped and went cold. She stared at the phone as if it were a videophone, as if she could examine her caller's face to verify whether it was really Christophe. "I have to…"

Stack looked as if he was about to plead with her to let the call go, but then he inclined his head, courteous once again. Businesslike and polite. "Would you like to use my office?"

She shook her head, her thoughts disturbed by the persistent buzzing. "No, I—" She stumbled though the doorway and into the lobby.

"I'll call you," Stack promised.

"Don't," she said shortly.

With a look of mingled shame and regret, he nodded again and shut the door. Alone in the foyer, except for Stack's receptionist, who sat at the far end and tried not to look too curious, she picked up the call.

"Yes, Christophe." She was deliberately curt, to cover up

the fact that her heart was thumping. Whenever he made contact, it was usually not good news.

"Ah, I was beginning to think I had the wrong number. How is *ma femme?*"

"I'm not your wife anymore," she reminded him.

"Very true, and very sad," he replied, with regret that would have been convincing if she didn't know what a good liar he was. "How are you anyway?"

"Busy."

"Good. I'm glad you find fulfillment in taking food to rich people." The sarcasm was only lightly masked.

"I'm not—" She stopped. She didn't need to update Christophe on her recent career developments. It was his fault she'd had to make those changes in the first place. If he'd stood up to his responsibilities, she wouldn't be scrambling to pay her bills, and her daughter's. Speaking of which…

"How's my little cabbage?"

"Your little cabbage is just fine, no thanks to you," she responded sharply. "She'd be a lot better if you'd send her payments through." Although a month had passed since the divorce, she'd yet to receive an alimony payment. She could live with that. She was a big girl; she could pay her own bills. But on top of that, he was easily five months behind on child support. He was stiffing his own daughter. That, she couldn't forgive.

There was a delicate pause on the line, and then Christophe said, with deceptive nonchalance, "Ah, yes. The payments. I've been meaning to talk to you about that."

"What's there to talk about? Bee's your daughter. Your flesh and blood—"

"Béatrice. Her name is *Bé-a-trice*. My mother, God rest her, would be tumbling in her grave—"

"Spinning," Shani corrected automatically.

"Spinning, tumbling, whatever you wish." He dismissed the finer points of the English language with a snarl. "She would not be happy to hear how you make ridiculous her name. You Americans, never taking the time to say something properly. Cutting good Christian names short for your own lazy convenience—"

"Listen, *Chris*, whatever you called for, why don't you just spit it out?"

"Ah, yes. Always rushing, you Americans—"

"You didn't mind me being American when I was helping you get your green card. Now, unless you're calling to let me know you're about to wire me the child support you owe…"

In his sigh, there was trouble. "Ah, sadly, no…"

Shani tried not to grind her teeth. "I talked to my lawyer about this…"

"Ah, yes. Mr. Dorian Black. He has called me a few times. Odd name, *ce mec,* but charming."

"And did he tell you you're obligated to send me—"

"He made me to understand this, yes, but sadly, I cannot."

"You can't…"

"I'm a little bit *fauché* these days. Er, low on funds, you understand?"

The tenuous hold she had on her patience snapped. "Low on funds? You run a thriving business, Christophe, and we're talking about your daughter's well-being here. You helped make her—you've got to help take care of her. I'm not in the mood to listen to you try to weasel out—"

"I have no wish to weasel out, as you say. I am calling to offer you a deal."

"Deal? A court passed judgment on you. There's no more dealing to be done!"

"You'll be interested in this one, I think." Christophe's voice, now stripped of the careless charm that Shani had once found so attractive, was cool and cutting. It was the voice of a man who'd been dealt a winning hand. It scared her. "I'm a photographer, yes? An artist."

Cold dread crept in.

"I make money from the photos I take, *oui*?"

Her breaths, shallow and sharp, were accompanied by a piercing pain under the ribs. "Get to the damn point."

"The point is I've been made an offer for some beautiful photographs of you. The last set, they were quite well received, no? Well, these…perhaps you'll remember them. Mementos of that wonderful night at Les Salines Beach. We swam naked, not even caring if there was anyone around to see. There was this beautiful, low moon, filling up the sky. And I took many photos of my beautiful goddess wife. Wearing nothing but a fine dust of silver sand…ah, I'm hard with the memory…"

Her gasp was painful and hoarse. "You wouldn't!"

"But you know I would. It's a good offer, from a popular magazine. And this one, it is not just for sale in France. It will be available for the world to admire. You'll be famous again."

The thought made her woozy. If Christophe published the photos, it would start again. Knowing glances from men; slow, salacious smiles. That grotesque sensation of walking around naked, even when she was fully dressed. And this time, not just in the French territories, but right here in the States. "Those are my images! I have a right to say whether they can be used or not!"

"What are you going to do? Sue me again?"

He was right. The lawsuit she'd filed against him after he'd unleashed the first set of photos without her permission was floundering in a sea of international red tape and protocols. Christophe was across an ocean, in another jurisdiction, and it would take years to arrive at a resolution.

She tilted forward, resting her face against the cool glass of the window. Down below, normal people were rushing about their normal lives. Up here, a bomb had gone off in hers. "What's your deal?"

"The deal is you excuse me from these payments. In return, I give you the photos."

"How many payments?"

"But all of them, my dear."

"For life? You want to give up on your daughter for life? What about school? What about college?"

"Oh, don't be dramatic. I'm giving up on no one. She will receive generous gifts on her birthday and Christmas. It will be up to you to manage them properly. But I am not a man who enjoys being directed by the courts, you understand? So I am saying this—you relieve me of this financial burden, to our daughter and to yourself—"

"No alimony either?"

"—and the photographs are all yours."

"You freaking jerk!" She wanted to throw the phone to the ground, smash it under her heel. Damn Christophe; each time she spoke to him, she was that much closer to a stroke. "I'm warning you, Chris…"

"You will call me later. This, it's not over." The line went dead.

Call him later? On Elliot's birthday? Calling Christophe was the last thing she wanted to do. And those photos! Did she remember them? He had to be joking. They'd gone back to Martinique on their honeymoon, and after a night of slamming down *petits ponches,* a sweet, rum-based drink that had a kick like a mule, they'd found themselves at Les Salines Beach. They'd swum naked, letting the warm Caribbean Sea lap at their skin from below and the moonlight wash over them from above. They'd crawled into a *pirogue,* a wooden fishing boat that had been dragged up above the water line, and made love, limbs enmeshed in the fishing nets. Translucent fish scales sticking to their skin like large, shining sequins. Then Christophe had pulled out his ever-present camera…

She felt like throwing up. He wouldn't really publish those! *Would he?*

Chapter 12

Elliot couldn't understand it. All the elements of a perfect evening were there: Shani looked fantastic, and she smelled even better; the Indian restaurant she'd chosen had a kind of exotic elegance that made every spicy, perfumed bite of food an experience. Most of all, tonight he was ready to tell her he loved her. He'd struggled with the decision for a while; it was the kind of thing which, once said, couldn't be unsaid.

Shani was so different from the women he'd known. She had a glow deep down inside her that left him in awe; her complexity, her humanity, her love for her child, her fragility, her sexual appetite, all of this combined to make a heady potion of which he'd drunk deeply. He was way past his limit, but he wanted to drink more.

And so, tonight, he'd been planning to tell her.

But something wasn't right, only for the life of him, he couldn't figure out what. She smiled whenever he caught her eye, chatted and proclaimed the food delicious, although she didn't eat much of it. But there was a shadow of worry in her eyes, a barrier between them made up of pained knowledge on her part, and ignorance on his. It was like seeing a mote, a movement in the corner of his eye, but every time he turned to look at it head-on, it was gone.

To make things worse, two dipsticks one table over just couldn't keep their eyes off his date.

"Know those guys?" he eventually had to ask.

She frowned elaborately. "Who?"

"The two idiots who've been staring at you and nudging each other since they sat down. Giggling like morons. Don't tell me you haven't seen them."

She glanced immediately over at the table in question. Two foreign-looking men, with their Euro-styled button-down shirts and pallid, hawkish faces, were putting away platters of chappatis and an assortment of curries, drinking fruit wine from brass bowls and talking too loudly. They caught her glance and broke into grins. One lifted his bowl to her in salute and slowly brought it to his lips, in what the fool probably thought was a seductive gesture.

"Know them?" he repeated.

Shani sipped on her tamarind juice, as if she was buying herself time. "I...uh...don't think so."

"They seem to know you."

She lifted her beautiful shoulders. "Maybe I...served them at a party," she managed weakly.

Maybe the Pope was taking up Buddhism. Elliot sighed. Shani had hinted there was more of the evening to come. If dinner wasn't working out, maybe they should just move on to phase two. But before they did... He put his hand in his pocket, withdrew a small box and then slid it across the table with a smile. "Happy unbirthday."

She opened it carefully, half smiling, throwing him

inquiring glances. He leaned forward to watch her take the gift from the box, as if he hadn't been the one to put it there in the first place. It was a fine gold chain with a polished, teardrop-shaped piece of amber dangling from the middle link. The glow of the amber matched the delight in her eyes. "Elliot! It's gorgeous!"

It was the first real pleasure he'd seen in her all evening. "Glad you like it."

"But…why? It's your birthday, not mine!"

"I just wanted you to have it." He tried to sound casual, even though the gift was only a precursor to his confession of love, a tap on the door through which he hoped to enter.

"Oh, and all I got you were stupid concert tickets and a whole bunch of…*car products!* I'm a terrible shopper! I give awful presents."

"Relax. They were great presents. I love Wyclef and I'm dying to see him live. And you know how much my car means to me. She'll be glowing like a diamond when I'm done. Matter of fact—" he gave her an impish smirk "—maybe this weekend you can come over and help me wash her. You bring the bikini. I'll handle the suds."

She looked somewhat mollified but still rueful. When he realized she wasn't going to put the necklace on, he got up, took it from her hands and tenderly placed it around her neck. He loved the smell of her; it radiated upward in warm waves as he bent over. He could feel the pulse beat at her throat. For triple-bonus points, from this vantage point he could see all the way down the neckline of that delightfully brief dress of hers.

He pressed a kiss on the crown of her head and then let his lips slide to her ear. Now was the time. She was warm and glowing and ready. He brought his mouth close. "Shani," he began.

Then, a presence at his elbow. Two presences; neither of them welcome. One of them cleared his throat. "Excuse me."

Elliot's spine snapped erect, and he spun around like a dog that, about to take the first bite from its bowl, was suddenly aware of two mangy pot hounds on its turf. It was those two damn fools from the next table. On the outside, they were plastered with persistent grins. On the inside, they were plastered with Mumbai liquor.

"Help you fellas?" Elliot made no secret of his irritation and dislike.

They shouldered past him as if he were merely a bystander, an obstacle on their quest. "Mademoiselle? My partner and I, we are wondering… It is you, is it not?"

Shani craned her neck to stare at them, wild-eyed and trapped. "I don't…I think you must be mistaken…"

The thinner one, brushing a pretentious bang out of his colorless eyes, insisted, "*S'il vous plaît,* we are simply…how you say…fans. Admirers. We wish only a moment…"

The smaller, younger man stepped closer. "We wish just to kiss your pretty hand. *C'est tout.* And an autograph. A souvenir, yes?" He snatched up the dessert menu from beside Shani's plate. "Here, you sign this. Then we go…"

Elliot shifted, partially blocking Shani from their view. He was in full-on territorial-dog mode, ready to go for the nearest exposed throat. "I asked if I could help you gentlemen." Not only had they killed his moment, but they were imposing their presence on his woman, and she didn't look as if she was enjoying it.

The older one flashed an impolite, foreign-looking hand gesture, which was so ridiculous that Elliot would have laughed if he wasn't three seconds away from kicking ass. "*Mon ami,* we only wish a moment. We want to let your lady know we are…admirers. You must be, too, *oui?*"

The other man's leer exposed bad teeth. "You are used to the attention, *ma belle, non?*"

Elliot was as confused as he was angry. "Shani, what's this about?"

Her eyes darted from one man to the next, as if she was afraid of imminent assault. "Nothing, Elliot! They're mistaken!"

The younger fool wasn't taking no for an answer. "You sign this, *ma belle,* and then we leave." He waved the menu in her face as if he was chasing flies.

For Elliot, the battle trumpet had sounded. He grabbed the hand holding the menu and twisted hard, bringing it around the man's back and yanking up so sharply that it touched the back of his neck. The Frenchman wriggled and twisted to prevent the ugly popping sound that would come next, as his humerus left its socket. He grunted and let the menu fall.

"Call her your *belle* again," Elliot suggested. "Try it."

The tall, dark maître d' in a gold-embroidered *kurta* and turban hurried over. "Sir! You can't…" His curved, waxed moustache twitched in agitation.

"Nothing to say?" Elliot taunted his victim. He cast a challenge at the man's companion. "You?"

The man threw up his hands, obviously not wanting to get blood on a perfectly good shirt. "No, *monsieur.*" He glanced at Shani and then back at Elliot. "We offer you our apologies. We must be…eh…we have made mistake."

Elliot had the nasty, ugly feeling in his gut that there was no mistake at all, but that the guy would deny knowing his own grandmother if it would save him from a beatdown.

The Indian in the turban was hopping around, saying, "Sir! Sir!" The Frenchman he was currently maiming was almost sobbing, a humiliated pretzel.

"Elliot, please…" Shani begged.

Partly disgusted at his own reaction, and partly disappointed at being denied the opportunity to vent his puzzlement and frustration on the guy's face, Elliot let go. The pair darted back to their table, where they began to gather their things. Dinner was over prematurely for them.

And for him and Shani. Now that it was evident that the gold-plated cutlery was not about to go airborne, the maître d' began glowering at him. Shani was still sitting, looking trapped in the headlights. He sighed. "Let's go, sweetheart."

She fumbled for her purse, dropped it, picked up the spilled contents and then dug around for her money.

He didn't have time for that. "Never mind," he said shortly, and tossed a few bills on the table. He held out his hand to help her rise.

She did so, protesting. "It's your birthday, Elliot! I invited you out. I'm the one that's supposed to—"

"Forget it. You can get it next time. Let's get out of here."

"But it's your—"

He glanced at his watch. "Not much of it left, anyway. Come, honey, please."

To his relief, she let him take her hand, and they left with little more than an apologetic nod to the turbaned man supervising their departure.

Chapter 13

It was one of those evenings when you longed for one thing and one thing only: for it to be over. Shani closed her eyes, drowning in wordless misery, glad the room was dim, lit by nothing more than banks of candles and oil lamps. Elliot was lying next to her, within arm's reach, but he wasn't saying much.

It had seemed like a fabulous idea: a couple's massage, Elliot and her lying side by side, slick with warm, sweet-scented oil, having their cares soothed away under the hands of two professional masseuses. Could anything be more sensual? Knowing Elliot, an hour of being pampered and stroked would have left him in such a state of arousal that they wouldn't have made it all the way back to his place—which was why she'd booked them a room in the hotel right next door to their spa. They'd have dashed, laughing, stress free and horny, to throw themselves onto the thickly carpeted floor just inside their hotel room door.

Round one would have taken place right there, round two on the bed and, if she was lucky, round three in the vicinity of the bathtub.

That was the plan, of course, before the hell-bound handbasket had drawn up to her table, and two grinning, drunken imps had shoved her inside.

Now Elliot was angry, hurt, bewildered and a whole lot more. He'd said nothing on the way over; as a matter of fact, he seemed determined that she should be the one to do the talking. And, to give him credit, he was right. She *should* say something. But what? That the Bozo Brothers had caught her with her pants down—literally—and they'd liked what they'd seen? And while they were on the subject, there was a fresh batch of photos poised to hit the newsstands in the U.S., just in case the entire planet hadn't seen her naked the first time?

That'd go down well.

And for this to happen now, just when she was beginning to discover how deeply her feelings for him ran. It was enough to make her sick.

"Did you hear yourself?" Elliot asked from beside her.

"Huh?"

"You just groaned like you were at the bottom of a well, with nobody around for miles to get you out."

Had she? "Oh."

"I'm around, though."

"You're...?"

"Around. To get you out." The small, beautiful Thai woman in the silk sarong who was delicately stroking her fingertips at the base of Elliot's neck moved to his lower back and hips. She could now see his face clearly. It was sober, serious. "I'm here if you want to tell me about it."

"Tell you about what?" she stalled.

His mouth twisted. "No more games, Shani, please. This is me. You have to say something sometime. Why not now?"

"What do you want to hear?"

"You can start with those two guys. And the autograph."

Decisions. Life's journey was guided, in part, by the decisions a person made, the path he or she chose. Somewhere, right now, someone was making the decision to take a nation to war. A couple was deciding to make love for the first time, another to end their love. Someone was deciding to have a baby, to start a new life, and someone else, for whatever ugly reason, was deciding to relieve someone else of his or her life. Decisions.

She turned over, onto her back, even though her masseuse was nowhere near done with her shoulders. The woman clucked her disapproval but simply rearranged the towel and went to work on Shani's front.

The yellow glow of the scented candles and sweet-oil lamps made a tapestry of shadows on the ceiling and walls. The scent of mandarin and lemongrass oil filled her nostrils, calming her enough for her to begin her confession. *Here goes nothing.* "Those guys…."

"Yes?"

"I guess they did…know me. If you could call it that. They don't *know me,* know me. We've never met. But they've seen me before." *Slow down,* she told herself. *You're babbling.*

"Where?"

Her masseuse was talented, but right now her hands didn't come close to easing the knots of tension and dread forming in her shoulders. "There was this magazine…."

"What kind of magazine?" he asked after a too-long pause.

"The kind...oh—" even her face hurt now "—the kind that publishes photos of women—naked women—in, um, compromising positions."

"You're a *porn* star?" Elliot jerked into a sitting position, his towel falling away. Their masseuses, as trained as they might have been to ignore even the most intimate of conversations while they were working, abandoned all pretense of being oblivious. They both stopped and gawked at Shani, identical cupid's-bow mouths agape.

She sat up too, anxious to defend herself. "I'm not a porn star! It was just that once, and in any case, I didn't plan it."

"You didn't plan to take your clothes off and parade around butt-naked in a magazine?"

"No!"

"Did they fall off on their own?"

"Did what fall...?"

"Your clothes."

"No, I took them...Elliot, listen. Those photos were private. I let my husband take them...."

He rolled his eyes and groaned. "Oh, great. Christian again. Guy sure has a way of ruining my—"

"Christ-*ophe!*"

"I told you, I don't give a...look, Shani, let's just slow down and back up, okay? You say your husband took these photos—"

"*Ex*-husband," she cut in bitterly.

"Ex. Which is fine with me. You say he took these photos..."

"He's a photographer. He does that for a living. But these photos were private. Between him and me, understand? We were fooling around, making love, and..."

Elliot grunted as if he'd been pierced under the ribs with a sharp object.

"Married couples do that, Elliot!"

"I know. I just don't need to hear about it all the time! I don't want to hear about you and any guy, past, present, future…"

Under other circumstances, his jealousy would have been flattering. "He asked me to pose for him, and I did. I thought it was exciting. I thought maybe we'd have something to look back on when we were old, to remind us of being young and in love and…"

"Jeez, Shani!"

"You want to hear this or not?"

He bowed his head and pressed his lips together. "Sorry. Go on."

By now both masseuses had given up on trying to get either of them to stay quiet long enough to finish their massage, and so they had retreated to the corner, letting what was left of the hour dribble through their inactive fingers, indulging in the real-life drama unfolding. Shani considered paying them what was due and asking them to scoot, but she didn't have the energy. So she pretended they weren't there and continued. "Well, things got bad fast between Christophe and me. And he decided to sell them. He got good money for them, but I'm sure he enjoyed humiliating me even more."

"So there're explicit, naked pictures of you out there. In some girlie mag."

"A French magazine. Not generally available in the States. Although, you know, it's a global village—every now and than, stuff slips across borders."

"Great."

He looked so horrified, so disapproving, she decided, dammit, she wasn't going to let him grab the moral upper hand. "Oh, don't act like butter won't melt. Don't tell me you've never read one of those mags. Don't tell me you haven't ogled a naked butt or two…."

"'Course I have. I'm a guy! But that doesn't mean I like knowing my girlfriend was splashed all over one of them."

"That's a double standard."

"It is. But we men are creatures of double standards. Live with it."

"Well," she retorted, "there are photos of me out there, and thousands of guys have looked at them and enjoyed them, just like you've looked at other women. *You* live with *that*!"

"That's asking plenty."

"It's the best I can do."

Still sitting on the massage table, he drew his knees up and rested his elbows on them, staring at the flickering lights on the wall. Shani waited, watching him. It was like watching the short hand move around a clock face.

Eventually, he asked, "That why you stopped lecturing?"

Perceptive, she thought. "Apparently the university takes the morality clause in its contracts very seriously."

Elliot closed his eyes and focused so intently on nothing at all that Shani half expected him to levitate. "People will forget," he said finally. "It'll fade with time."

She could have left him with that shred of reassurance, but she'd committed to telling him the truth, even if it put their relationship on the line. With shards of glass tearing at her insides, she added, "There're more photos."

His eyes were open, alert. "What?"

"Christophe. He's got more photos. And he's planning to sell them, unless I waive my right to alimony and to Bee's payments."

"He told you this?"

"Yes."

"When?"

"Today. He called me, told me he'd had an offer. Said I could forget about getting paid, or see myself in print again." She laughed bitterly.

"So that's what you've been stewing in all evening," he said thoughtfully.

"I guess." Part of it, at least—she hadn't forgotten Stack's awkward fumble and her resulting joblessness, but she resolved to let that part simmer on the back burner. Elliot didn't deserve any more thrown at him tonight. "Sorry I ruined your birthday."

He shrugged it off as if it was the least of his worries. "These photos…" he began slowly and painfully.

"…Are as bad as you think they are."

"Can't you sue him? Stop him?"

"I tried that the last time. It's all tangled in red tape. And how'd I even begin to pay for another lawsuit? He hasn't even coughed up the money he owes to pay for the divorce."

"I could lend you—"

"Don't even think about it."

His face twisted in frustration. Then he looked as if it had only just occurred to him that they were performing before a live audience. He turned to the two young women. "Ladies, would you excuse us?"

Disappointed, but well trained, the women bowed elaborately and exited soundlessly, leaving them alone at last.

Elliot hopped down from his table and began to get dressed, angrily dragging on his clothes.

Shani watched him anxiously. "Elliot…?"

"Couldn't you have kept them on?"

"'Scuse me?"

"Your panties," he grated. "Would that have been too much to ask?"

She was off the table like a shot and standing before him, naked as a jaybird and mad as a hissing cobra. "How dare you question my morals! Who the hell are you to make comments about what I chose to do in the confines of my marriage? You judge me on the basis of a few stupid photos? You're as sexist as your father!"

Elliot froze. "My father knows about this?"

Ah, crap. Loose lips sure did sink ships. She clamped her jaw shut, but it was too late.

"He's seen them, hasn't he? Stack's seen you naked."

She nodded, waiting for heaven to come crashing down around her ears.

He continued yanking on his clothes. "Get dressed. We're leaving."

"Elliot…"

"Put your clothes on, Shani, please! I need to get out of here before these walls…"

"Okay, okay!" She found her pretty new wine-colored dress and miserably pulled it over her head. She found her panties and put those on, too, but not without some irony.

When they were both dressed and she'd left adequate payment on the side table, he grasped her elbow and ushered her outside. After the warmth of the room and the blood-stimulating effects of the massage, the cold air was an all-over slap. Shani shivered. Elliot opened his car door, allowed her to sit and slammed it so hard the car shuddered.

She wrapped her arms around herself as he started the engine and peeled off without even waiting for it to warm up. As they passed the fancy hotel where she'd booked a room in anticipation of an uninhibited night of birthday-present sex, she sighed.

The silence was agonizing. But when he eventually spoke, ten minutes later, she began to wish he hadn't. "So you and Stack have been keeping secrets from me."

"Just the one," she managed to lie.

"Oh, and it's just a tiny one, huh?"

"What's bothering you more? The secret itself, or the fact that Stack was in on it?"

"Both. And it's not just the secret—it's what it means."

"And what's it mean?"

"It means that my girlfriend, a woman I thought I could trust, thinks I can't handle the knowledge…oh, goddammit. I haven't a clue what you think about me."

I think I love you, she thought achingly. *But that's a moot point now.*

"What do you want me to be for you? Because I want to be your man. I want to matter to you!"

"You do," she protested. *More than you know.*

"Then maybe you could share important things in your life with me, instead of thinking I can't handle them. You keep shutting me out." Before she could protest, he added bitterly, "And your ex-husband! No matter what I do, the guy just creeps into our life. He's like a bad smell, or a stain on the wall I can't get rid of."

What could she say about Christophe? She felt as though she were adrift in a boundless sea trying to get as far away as she could, but with every stroke, he wrapped himself around her legs like seaweed. It was frustrating, dealing with all the muddied emotions left behind by a collapsed marriage. She could imagine how hard it was on Elliot.

They crossed town in record time. As always, the streets of Catarina were alive. Elliot pulled up in front of Old Seoul, and Shani opened the door and got out before he could open it for her. She stood at the curb, watching him warily over the top of the low-slung car. Was this it, then?

Was this how it ended, on a cold public street, with so many things yet unsaid?

Deep inside, her soul groaned. She couldn't let her savior, her dark, complex, compassionate angel, unfurl his wings and leave her life. "Elliot," she began, but stalled.

His eyes were unreadable, his arms stiff at his sides. He glanced upward at her windows; the lights inside were off. She'd arranged for Bee to spend the night downstairs with the Paks. His jaw moved as if he'd made an important decision. "Go get some sleep."

"But you can't…" She wanted to throw herself onto the hood of the car, make a complete ass of herself in front of whoever was watching, anything to stop him from leaving.

He yanked open his door. "Get some sleep, Shani. You need it. Me too."

As he started the engine, she jerked away from the car. The window on the passenger side was wound down, his face framed in it, a frightening tableau of anger, longing, uncertainty and fatigue. She wanted to call his name again, but she felt too foolish.

"Sleep," was all he said, and peeled away, leaving the stink of burned rubber behind.

Chapter 14

Four agonizing, excruciating days. The phone was so silent, Shani had to convince herself—sometimes out loud—there was nothing wrong with it, and she wasn't doing the situation much good by constantly picking it up and checking for a dial tone. For that matter, text messages weren't getting gobbled up as they arced midair from Elliot's phone to hers: he simply wasn't sending any. Ditto for email, carrier pigeon and any other form of communication he might employ, but didn't.

For Bee's sake, she tried to act as if everything was normal. Every afternoon after day care she devised some form of entertainment that delayed their return to the apartment. One day, they took a trip to the zoo; the other, they enjoyed a Mommy and Me session at the library. She laughed when Bee expected her to, and pretended, pretended, pretended.

But not even a three-year-old was buying her act. After

Bee informed her that her red-rimmed, dark-circled eyes made her look like a raccoon, she bought eyedrops and a concealer stick. But concealer couldn't hide Elliot's absence. The fact that Elliot hadn't blessed Bee's little life with gorilla grunts and candy was a circumstance she felt honor-bound to remind her mother of—ten times a day. The inquisition became a ritual that left Shani exhausted and close to tears:

"Where's Elliot?"

"I don't know, honey."

"Why isn't he here?"

"Sorry, sweetheart, but I don't know."

"Is he sick?"

"I don't think so."

"He's sick! We have to go bring him soup!"

"I don't think he's sick, Bee."

"Is he mad at me?"

"I promise you, he's not mad at you."

"He mad at *you*?"

"Eat your dinner."

Gina was even worse. It hadn't taken the teenager long to figure out something was up, and, naturally, it was Shani's fault, because her newfound idol just had to be the injured party. After all, the man was cooler than Kanye. Since Gina had no reason to be upstairs, because Shani didn't need babysitting services, she was content to position herself in one of the restaurant's open windows, or to hover around the stairs, to glower at Shani as she passed, the way only a teenager could.

Shani was glad to have two other people's feelings to worry about, because it gave her an excuse not to focus on her own. The rawness, the desolation, the gnawing feeling of failure were too much to bear.

She sat on her bed, grateful for the silence while Bee was

in day care. The bedsheets were rumpled and smelled of baby lotion and the handful of jellybeans scattered among them. But her thoughts were not of Bee.

The first time she and Elliot had made love here, she'd said some nonsense about not believing in love. He'd insisted it was out there; it only had to find her. Now it had, she thought miserably, just long enough for her to have a taste of what she was missing. Then it went on its merry way, like a butterfly that didn't know it had caused a cyclone with the flap of its wings.

There had to be a way to fix this. He couldn't stay mad at her forever…could he? Even if he was still mad, this calamity had been her fault, and the onus was on her to make reparations. She needed to go over there. Apologize. Ask for another chance.

She got up, found her purse and shoes, and then stopped at the mirror for a few seconds to take in her reflection. She looked a mess: mussed hair, dark-circled eyes and an aura of fatigue that slapped a few extra years on her face. She should try to fix it—but the fire in her burned too hot.

She careened downstairs, past Old Seoul and its strong smells, glad Gina was in school and she'd be spared the hurt, dirty looks. Maybe she should talk to the girl, explain that life wasn't as easy as it was in the rom-coms Gina loved.

But right now, she needed one thing…. She almost tripped on the last step, but she righted herself. Her train of thought skipped like a scratched CD, but she found where she'd left off. Right now, she needed to see… She slammed into a brick wall someone had put up at the base of her steps, smack in the middle of the sidewalk. It was solid and unyielding and knocked the wind out of her. Her bag flew from her hands and thudded onto the sidewalk. She stooped and reached for her purse. The wall did the same.

Then her clouded, agitated brain realized it wasn't a piece of concrete at all. It was…

"Elliot!"

He handed her back her purse, his face sober. "Hey."

She knew she was breathing, but the air in her lungs wasn't doing her any good. "Hey," she managed to say.

She examined his face. There was something in the set of his mouth, a tension in his jaw, that gave him faint creases at the corners of his lips, hairlines that hadn't been there before. His eyes were shadowy from lack of sleep, pale purple blotches stealing their sparkle. She thought for a second that the two of them would probably make a killing in vaudeville as some kind of singing and dancing raccoon act, which just went to show that insomnia really did send a body crazy.

He helped her up from her crouched down position, and they stood on the sidewalk, contemplating each other and their next move. "Going somewhere?" he asked.

She had been going somewhere, hadn't she? "I was, uh, going to see you."

The smile that spread across his face ironed out the creases. "Really?"

She nodded vigorously.

"Why?"

"I had to see you. I…" Courage, courage! "Bee's been asking for you nonstop. She thinks you're mad at her."

"I'll tell her I'm not, when next I see her."

"And Gina," she prattled on, "oh, Gina! She's been giving me the evil eye the whole time."

He was noncommittal, leaving it up to her to take the initiative. "Teenagers are like that. She'll come 'round."

Shani wasn't placing any bets. "She thinks it's my fault this is…over."

His face softened, becoming tender and concerned. "It was never over, sweetheart. Did you think it was?"

"Did I...Elliot, we parted in anger. I haven't heard from you in four days. What'd you expect me to think?"

He scratched his head sheepishly. "I know. I needed... time. Space. It's a lot to deal with."

She tried to explain, choosing her words carefully. "You have to understand—what happened, happened. A long time ago, way before I met you..."

"That wasn't the hard part."

"I know. It was the..." It was hard to get the word out. She started again. "It was the trust. And I'm sorry. I promise, I..." She put her hand on his arm, the first contact she'd had with him in days. The warmth and strength made her want to curl up against him, bury her face in his jacket, but she knew the danger wasn't over yet. She'd have to tread carefully, until she found herself on more solid ground.

"Elliot," she said slowly, "I'm sorry I hurt you. I'm sorry I didn't trust you enough to tell you. I will never, ever—"

He cut her off with a kiss. The taste of his lips, the scent of him, made her feel as if she'd stumbled home after being away too long. It was like staggering down the gangplank of a ship, still dizzy from the tossing of the waves, and falling to her knees to press her lips to the soil of her motherland. He placed one hand on her lower back, at the waistband of her jeans, and slipped the other between them to press it flat against her belly, closing a circuit of warmth that coursed through her like a current.

"I missed you," he breathed.

Her voice was muffled. "Me, too. Don't leave me hanging like that ever again."

"I won't, love." He kissed her again.

What'd he just call her? She tore herself away from

his lips so she could look up at him, her eyes full of questions.

He nodded slowly in confirmation. His mouth looked as if it was struggling to keep his smiles in. "I wanted to tell you that night. At the restaurant. I'd started, actually, when those two jackasses came over…" He laughed ruefully. "The only thing that got between me and killing them was the knowledge of what'd happen to a pretty guy like me in prison."

She laughed. On the inside, joy was bubbling up. Elliot loved her. This man who believed in love, and had sworn to her that it would find her some day, loved her. She wondered if doing gleeful backflips on the sidewalk would be inappropriate. Maybe four or five or so, as far as the curb. Anything more than that would be showing off.

"I wanted to tell you—I changed my mind…."

He was wary, not quite getting her. "About what?"

"About love being just a fantasy…."

"Uh-huh?"

"Well, I guess it was a pretty stupid idea."

"I could have told you that."

"You did." Right before he'd tossed her on the bed like a bale of hay and done things to her with his mouth that made her forget her own name. "And you were right."

"I usually am."

She punched him on the shoulder and was immediately sorry she did. She'd have been better off trying to put her hand through a pile of bricks. "Ouch!"

"Serves you right." He took her hand, kissed each knuckle and then slowly slipped her little finger into his mouth, engulfing it in wetness, reminding her just how warm his mouth could be. How skilled it could be. Deep inside her, warm moisture began to flow.

"Elliot, you're making it hard…"

"You can say that again!"

She considered hitting him again but thought better of it. "That's not what I meant. You're making it hard for me to say…what I have to say…."

He stopped sucking at once. "What do you have to say?"

"That I…" she took a deep, fortifying breath "…love you."

He was grinning like an idiot. "There, now. Don't you feel better?"

"That's not the accepted response, Elliot!"

"Sorry, honey, I couldn't resist. You should see the look on your face…."

"Well, I'm glad you're amused. I lay my heart bare to you…"

"And a beautiful heart it is. Not to mention the packaging it comes in." He let one hand idly caress her left breast.

"…and all you can do is make jokes about it? I'm telling you, mister—"

"Shani…"

"What?"

"I love you."

The words knocked the wind from her sails.

There was a clank behind her, the sound of the restaurant doors being flung open in readiness for the lunchtime crowd. Shani spun around. Mrs. Pak, dressed in the traditional garb she always wore, gave her the broadest of smiles and waved. Shani and Elliot waved back.

"Now, my dear," he said gravely, "you have two choices."

"Which are?"

He held up one finger. "One, I could drag you into my car, roll up the windows, strip you down and help you steam up the glass. Which probably wouldn't do much for anyone's appetite, so I doubt the Paks would be thrilled."

"Probably not. What's behind door number two?"

He held up another finger and had the audacity to wiggle it suggestively. "Two, I drag you upstairs. After which the stripping-you-down scenario would probably be the same. With more room, of course."

She pretended to be uncertain. "I don't know. They both involve me getting dragged."

"We could revise that to a run, if you think you can keep up with me, because if you can't, I'm starting without you."

The image veered between laughable and erotic. Erotic won out. She tapped him lightly on the shoulder. "Tag," she said. "You're it." And she beat him to the top of the stairs.

They made it as far as the couch but decided to forgo the luxury of being naked. That was just too much time to waste. They kissed until they should have been tired of it, but weren't. He slid his hand up under her blouse, stroking her inflamed skin. His fingers brushed against something smooth and hard. He rolled up her top to find the amber pendant he'd given her nestled snugly between her breasts.

"You're still wearing it," he said wonderingly.

"Never took it off."

He examined it as if he'd never seen it before, then, pulling down the cup of her bra to expose her breast, lightly rubbed the blunt edge of it against the tip of her nipple.

"Jerk," she gasped.

He toyed with her for a few moments more and then let the pendant fall back into its nesting place. "That's it," he announced.

"That's what?"

"Appetizer's over. Time for lunch." He yanked on her jeans, trying to open them, but fumbled in his haste. "You put a padlock on this?"

"Only a zipper. Which you'd be able to open if you had a little patience."

"Patience?" He looked at her as if she'd said a swear-word in church. "Could you just get the damn thing off?"

She was only too happy to comply.

What a difference love makes, Shani thought dreamily, with the tiny corner of her mind that still retained rational thought. Her body was familiar with the way Elliot moved inside her, but this time, every stroke was a confession of how much he felt. Their bodies shared a conversation, separate from any their owners could have had verbally. Their lips and limbs, nipples and bellies whispered back and forth between them, exchanging confidences, making promises.

They lay on the couch, squeezed together for lack of space, sweaty bodies sticking to the fabric. Trying to slow their breathing again, because if their hearts kept racing it would surely kill them both. He let his heavy head rest on her shoulder. She stroked his short hair. "I miss it being long and messy," she said.

"Huh. Now you tell me."

There was something she needed to know, and she was half-afraid that asking would rip apart the fragile web holding them together. But her mind wouldn't rest until she had the answer. "Elliot?"

He was half dozing. "Mmm?"

"Did you go online and look for my pictures?"

He hesitated, but only for a fraction. "Yes."

"Find them?"

"Uh-huh."

Say something, dammit, she thought. When he didn't, she ventured, "What do you think?"

"I think your butt's even cuter now than it was then."

"Seriously, Elliot!"

He shifted so he could look at her. His thick brows were drawn. "I don't know, Shani. What do you want me to say? I don't like it, the idea of other guys looking at you like that, but I can live with it. I'm here, aren't I?"

"Yes. You are." It should be good enough for her. She toyed with the idea of asking him what he felt about his father, specifically, having seen them, but she decided that an open can of worms didn't make very good bedfellows. She was prepared to leave it at that.

He wasn't. He propped himself up on his elbows. "While we're on the subject…"

She struggled not to start hyperventilating again.

"I was thinking about the other set of photos. The one your ex has."

That wasn't where she was expecting him to go. "Yes?"

"We're going to get them."

"What?"

"We're going to Martinique, you and me, and we're going to find the sorry SOB and get your photos back. And let me go on record as renewing my original offer to beat him up."

She'd have smiled at the thought, if the idea wasn't so far-fetched. "Martinique? How're we going to—"

"I got tickets. We're leaving in the morning."

"You have—?"

"Right. In my jacket pocket." He looked around. "Where'd I put it?"

"Kitchen floor. But what about Bee? How'm I going to leave—?"

He lifted his hand placatingly. "It's okay. I talked to Mrs. Pak. Bee'll be fine."

That jolted her into a sitting position. "You did what?"

"It's only three days."

Was he just pretending to be clueless? "You made plans for my child without asking me?"

To his credit, he looked ashamed. "I didn't want you to say no. I knew you were mad at me, but I wanted to help, and this is the only way I knew how." He put his arms around her, and maybe it was that stupid magic way he had about him, to sway people around to his way of seeing things, but what he was saying almost made sense. Fly to the Caribbean. Find Christophe. Get the photos back. It almost sounded easy.

"Martinique, huh?" She closed her eyes, weighing her doubts. Bee would be okay; that wasn't a problem. It would mean facing Christophe again, and the prospect made her queasy. But Elliot would be there, the man who loved her. He'd have her back.

And ooh, Martinique. The Isle of Flowers. She could almost feel the sun on her skin. She'd be there in that sweet-scented, sunswept, magical place…with Elliot. Deciding. "Okay."

"Good girl."

Chapter 15

Elliot knew how to travel in style. They'd feasted on chicken colombo—spicy chunks of breast meat curried with chick peas, sautéed onions and coriander—arranged over a fluffy rice pilaf with raisins and slivered almonds. Dessert had been a rum-soaked concoction that smelled of bay leaves and tasted of cinnamon. It reminded Shani of the life she'd lived before the first set of photos had made her the pariah of the academic world. *Maybe when this is over,* she thought, *I could swallow my pride and find my place there again…*

Elliot was engrossed in a magazine, his hand resting lightly on her forearm, leaving her to the refuge of her own mind. They'd hopped a short flight from Santa Amata to JFK, switched planes and were in for a five-hour trip to Fort-de-France. It was a shame the flight was an evening one. It was way too dark to take advantage of the window seat Elliot had generously offered her.

She'd been to Martinique twice; once, on her own, for her research, and the second time with Christophe, for their honeymoon. Both times she'd flown in daylight, able to look out her window and soak up the glorious aquamarine of the Caribbean Sea. She was sure its exact shade was unmatched by any body of water in the world. Christophe used to brag that if heaven had a color, Caribbean blue was probably it.

Christophe. Even the sound of his name, spoken in the privacy of her thoughts, was enough to dispel the pleasant effects of the two glasses of *vin nouveau* she'd been served. It brought the image of his cruel, beautiful face to her mind, and the memory of their last conversation.

She'd let Elliot talk her into flying out to meet the man who'd made the past four years of her life miserable, to try to get back photos explicit enough to cause renewed humiliation. But she had no idea how to go about it, and she wasn't sure Elliot did, either. Did he think he could just walk up to Christophe and ask nicely? For Christophe, those photos meant money and freedom from his legal obligations to her and his daughter. He wasn't handing them over without a fight.

She threw Elliot a hasty glance. A fight. *God, tell me Elliot was joking when he talked about kicking the stuffing out of Christophe....* She groaned. She was taking her lover to meet her ex-husband on his home turf. Not to mention what it would be like for her, seeing the man she'd shared her life with, for the first time after so long. Did she have her head screwed on right?

The touch of Elliot's big hand, stroking her arm, pulled her away from her troubled thoughts, like a dying woman being yanked backward out of the dark tunnel into which her soul had fallen, away from the light.

"Penny for them," he offered softly. "Hell, you sounded

so sorrowful, sighing like that, I'm sure your thoughts are worth a lot more. I'm prepared to go as high as a buck." His kind, sad smile told her he had more than an inkling of what her thoughts were about.

Shani hesitated. She knew the effort it took for him to come with her, given that the mere mention of Christophe's name was enough to cause that vein in his forehead to swell to near bursting. Surely he didn't need to be regaled with details of her distress. Nope. You didn't need to know about guns to know it wasn't a bright idea to play with one that was loaded.

She answered vaguely. "I was just…hoping everything's gonna be okay, is all."

"It will be."

"Yes," she agreed without conviction.

He leaned over and looked into her eyes. His black ones held not a trace of doubt. "It will. I promise." He sighed. "It's killing me to see you like this. I'll do whatever it takes to help you solve your problem, but in the meantime, if you keep eating yourself up, you won't have any strength left when the moment's right. You need to lighten up." He looked around, as if trying to find something that would help. "Want me to call for more wine?"

She couldn't stop herself from smiling at that. "You kidding? We're a mile up. Know what that does to your ability to absorb alcohol? Another sip and I'll be flat on my back."

"Wouldn't mind having you flat on your back right now," he said and waggled his brows like Groucho Marx. "And since you mentioned it, being a mile high has its benefits…."

Shani watched as the laughter slipped away from his face, to be replaced by a glint that only the devil could have put there. "Come to think of it…"

He wasn't implying… But the flame that lit up his eyes told her he was. Shani was scandalized. "Don't be ridiculous! The Mile High Club—" She realized she was speaking too loudly, so she lowered her voice to a shocked whisper. "The Mile High Club isn't real. It's a myth!"

"No, it isn't."

"It's got to be. It's a fantasy made up by people who'd never have the guts to have sex parked in an *alley*, much less on a plane."

"Ah, that's where you're wrong, my dear." He kept the Groucho Marx impression going. "The club's real, and you don't even have to take a physical to join."

"How do you know? Have you joined?"

He gave an exaggerated sigh. "Not yet." His hand slid higher, slyly slipping along her side to caress her breast. The wine she'd had with dinner must have been pretty potent, because almost instantly, her skin was tingling.

"Ridiculous idea," she managed through clenched teeth.

"Brilliant idea," he argued. "Genius."

The sheer preposterousness of it made her giggle. "What, you're suggesting we wedge ourselves under the seat and go at it like bunnies?"

"No," he said in all seriousness, "I'm suggesting you precede me to the bathroom…"

She choked on a mixture of shock and anticipation. "In an airplane bathroom? There isn't enough room in there to swing a cat!"

"This is a first-class bathroom. There's enough room in there to do that and a whole lot more."

The idea was growing on her so fast, she had to kill it in its infancy. "Elliot, it's not possible…."

"It's eminently possible. We've got means, motive

and opportunity." The hand at her breast was still lazily, casually working its magic.

"Funny you should put it like that," she shot back. "It's probably an international offense."

"Probably," he agreed. The idea didn't faze him. "But think of the bragging rights. Fifty years from now, when you're rocking away on the porch, you'll have a secret to remind you of the time when you were young and daring and in your sexual prime."

She didn't want to tell him that that was pretty much the same argument Christophe had used to get her to pose buck nekkid for his camera.

Her eyes darted around. She was sure everyone in the cabin could tell exactly what they were considering, but most of their cabinmates were either sleeping or engrossed in the personal DVD players on the seat in front of them. "We're going to get caught," she protested.

"I'll be quick," he countered. Masculine pride made him add, "For a change."

She shut her eyes, but that only intensified the image of her and Elliot, with their clothes still on, pressed against each other in a cramped space, while the world went on, oblivious. Heat pooled between her thighs. She squirmed, and that was all he needed to see.

"Bathroom on the left," he instructed. "Wait sixty seconds, and then I'll be outside the door."

"Elliot, I—"

"Go."

She wondered if her walk looked casual enough, or if anyone looking at her could tell she was guilty as sin. She could feel her face flush. The idea was raunchy beyond belief. Just before making it to the bathroom, she had to squeeze past a flight attendant in the aisle: a willowy, dark-skinned Martiniquaise with perfect teeth and shocking gray contact lenses. Her close-fitting uniform, in colors that evoked a rich-hued Caribbean sunset, emphasized the way her hips swayed, as if she was listening to sensual *zouk* music through invisible earplugs. "Madame," the woman murmured as she went past. Shani mumbled a reply and tried not to scurry.

Serendipity! The bathroom was free. She slipped inside and locked the door. Eliot was precise; if he said he'd be there in sixty seconds, he would be. She counted the seconds off in her heated mind: "One chimpanzee, two chimpanzee…" She turned on the tap and splashed cool water on her face, checking her teeth, fussing with her hair. All the time telling herself just how absurd this all was.

Forty-six chimpanzee, forty-seven…

She popped open a tiny bottle of mouthwash and swigged it, wishing the alcohol content was a little higher. Fifty-eight chimpanzee, fifty-nine…

Her eyes roamed the bathroom, looking for hidden cameras, microphones, any suggestion that their escapade might end up as in-flight entertainment for the crew. She had to be out of her ever-lovin'—

Just as the sixty-fourth chimpanzee loped merrily on its way, there was a single, barely audible knock on the door. This was it. She could pretend she didn't hear him and pull her head down between her shoulders until he gave up and slunk back to his seat, or she could open up and risk being thrown off the flight in midair. Which? Her hand made up its own mind; it reached out and slid back the lock.

Casually, cool as an arctic spring, Elliot slipped inside and then rammed the lock home. "Take off your panties."

"What?"

"We've got about three minutes, baby. Take 'em off."

She didn't need to be told twice. In a single fluid motion

she bent forward and slid them down, yanked them over her shoes and tossed them onto the counter. He kissed her hard, his mouth tasting of wine. True, the bathroom was bigger in first class, but it still wasn't built for two. She could feel her bottom press against a panel of buttons, and she prayed that she didn't unwittingly set off one that would bring a flight attendant running.

Roughly, without speaking again, he put his hands on her hips and turned her around, so he was behind her—and they both faced the mirror. He yanked up the back of her short skirt, and she heard the sound of his zipper. With one knee rising between her thighs and pushing sideways, he parted her legs, and without preamble—as if they needed any—he slipped inside her. The effect was cataclysmic. A moan of shock and pleasure escaped her, loud enough to cause him to clap his hand over her mouth

"Shh…" he hissed.

She was trying. Lord, she was trying. But the feel of him inside her, huge with excitement, made her resolve weak. She felt his teeth scrape the back of her neck and sink in, and she was grateful that his hand was there to stifle her yowl of ecstasy. She lifted her eyes to his reflected ones, took in the sight of them, her top button undone, his other hand down the front of her blouse, torturing her nipples.

Mating like wolves.

Against her ear, Elliot's hot, excited mouth whispered every filthy thing. Shani could feel moisture roll down her thighs; she was wetter and more excited than she'd ever been in her life. With each powerful stroke she felt her body thud against the washbasin; it was loud enough, she was sure, to be heard above the steady hum of the engines. The rough fabric of their clothes awakened every nerve in their skin, and the buckle on the belt of his jeans punished the tender flesh of her bottom. She relished the idea of seeing bruises bloom there later.

High in the sky, above the silent and unknowing earth, she felt the thunderstorm of orgasm rolling in, threatening to blow her off her feet….

There was a pounding on the door, a rattling of the lock and a muffled, irritated voice on the other side. "Hello! In there!"

Elliot cursed but didn't stop. "Almost…there," he gasped.

Her heart was going crazy, pounding under his fingers. She was as close as he was. Twenty more seconds, she pleaded to the faceless intruder on the other side of the door. Ten!

There was a second voice now, a thickly accented one, and the knock was more commanding. "You weel open this door immediately! I insist!"

Elliot's eyes, still locked with hers, closed briefly, and when they opened again, they were filled with regret and thwarted passion. He pressed a tender kiss against her sweat-misted temple. "Jig's up, sugarcakes." He withdrew, leaving an aching space inside her.

"Open thees door!"

"One second!" he answered loudly.

Shani couldn't understand how he could sound so normal, when she was feeling as if she'd been trampled by a herd of stampeding moose. Her face was dripping, her hands shaking, and her legs sure as hell wouldn't be keeping her up on their own.

He hastened to rearrange the front of his jeans but didn't bother to tuck in his shirt. She snatched up a handful of paper towels and frantically dabbed away at her face. "Brace yourself," he advised as he made sure the hem of her skirt was straight. "Act nonchalant."

He had to be out of his mind.

The door clicked open. Shani couldn't even bear to look directly through it, but reflected in the glass she could see a diminutive woman with ancient, horn-rimmed glasses and her hair pulled into a scraggly bun. She looked like the tiny exorcist in *Poltergeist* who'd sworn the house was clean.

"See?" she shrilled at the flight attendant. "I told you there were two people in there!" It was the same attendant Shani had passed earlier, the elegant one with the spooky gray lenses. Shani wondered if it was possible to flush herself down the toilet behind her and be ejected over the Caribbean Sea, thus sparing herself the embarrassment.

Elliot filled the doorway, blocking Shani from two pairs of curious eyes. "My wife isn't feeling well," he apologized with just the right mixture of sincerity and concern. "I apologize if we inconvenienced you while I attended to her…needs."

The small woman's owlish eyes were puzzled, confused, striving to see past Elliot as she tried to determine if he was telling the truth. Her pursed lips told them she was sure he wasn't.

There was a *ding* nearby. The flight attendant said to the strange-looking little woman, "Madame, another bathroom has opened up. Maybe you would like to use that one?"

The woman looked disappointed, denied the chance to revel in the scandal a little longer, and slouched away. Elliot stood his ground in the doorway.

The flight attendant wasn't buying the yarn about feeling unwell. She folded her arms. "Monsieur, what you are doing is unsafe, illegal and, well…" she floundered, trapped in Elliot's unswerving gaze "…it is not allowed."

"I understand. I'm sorry if I've caused you any distress."

"I could have you arrested when we arrive in Fort-de-France. Would you like that?"

"I wouldn't like that at all," he said gravely. He ran one finger slowly, idly up the door frame, as if he was stroking a woman's arm. The woman watched it glide up and down, transfixed, like a cat tantalized by a feather in the breeze. From her vantage point, cowering against the washbasin, Shani watched, fascinated, as he hypnotized the woman. "You look like a kind person, and I know that, coming from the islands, you can understand how…passion…can make people do foolish things. You do understand, don't you?"

The gray eyes flickered toward Shani's flushed face, and her lips curved in an almost conspiratorial smile. "I imagine, *oui*."

"Then maybe we can keep this between us?"

"I think maybe we could." Her eyes were roaming Elliot's body now, and she shot Shani a look that said, *You go, girl.* "But you weel have to return to your seat at once, and we weel have no more of these nonsense, *comprendez?*"

He nodded, still smiling. "Understood."

"Bien."

As the woman turned to go, she caught sight of a thin strip of navy blue nylon puddled on the countertop. Shani's panties. The sight of it sent Shani into a coughing fit. Elliot snagged them and slipped them in his pocket as casually as a shoplifter. "Honeymoon," he said, and shrugged.

"Congratulations," the flight attendant murmured, more to Shani than to Elliot, and glided away.

They raced down the aisle like naughty children, bursting into fits of laughter as they tumbled into their seats. Now that it no longer seemed likely that she'd be experiencing firsthand the inside of a French prison, Shani was ebullient, jazzed on a potent cocktail of adrenaline and sexual arousal. She could barely catch her breath. Between ragged puffs of laughter, she managed to ask, "Did you see her face?"

"The flight attendant? Cute."

"Not her, dopey. The old lady. She was ready to have a coronary."

"Hardly. She was loving it. It's probably the best thing to happen to her since…forever."

Shani let her head flop back against the seat. Her body was still humming, hot and tingling. She needed a drink of water worse than the Lost Patrol. Elliot was right on it. He pulled a bottle of sparkling water from the pocket in front and held it to her lips. When she was done slaking her thirst, he finished the bottle. His eyes were ablaze. There were things pouring out of him in that single look that he'd never even verbalized.

Her breath wouldn't slow down. She couldn't look away from him even if she tried. No man had ever looked at her that way. It made her feel as if she could levitate.

"Congratulations," he said.

"On…?"

"On becoming the newest member of the club."

She was glad for the distraction, anything to reduce the intensity of that look. "Really think we're in?"

He frowned, puzzled. "What do you mean, are we in? There's only one entry requirement, and I think we just fulfilled it."

"Well, not completely. I mean, we didn't…you know."

He laughed. "Oh. Right. I see what you mean. Hmm." He looked as if he was actually turning it over in his mind. "You cold?"

He'd changed the subject on her so fast, her head spun. "What?"

"Maybe you should cover up," he suggested. He reached for her blanket and held it out to her.

Was she cold? She was radiating heat like a nebula. "I am certainly not—"

He broke the seal on the blanket and unwrapped it, and then he carefully arranged it so she was covered from neck to foot. And for the second time that night, he advised her, "Act nonchalant."

"Wha—? Elliot! Are you crazy? I'm *boiling*!" She was about to rip the blanket from around her when she felt it: his hand slipping under the blanket, sly and determined. Slinking up her body like a snake. Under the hem of her short skirt and up her thighs. By the time she had figured out his intent, contact was already made. She went bolt-rigid. "We…will…get…caught!" she hissed. "Again!"

"We will if you don't pipe down. Close your eyes. Make like you're asleep."

Sleep? Who could sleep—or pretend to be asleep—with what his fingers were doing to her? They were engulfed in wetness, and they knew exactly what to do. Stroking, stroking, stroking…

She was not going to look at him…she was not going to look at him…she was *not*…

His eyes were amused, mocking. She shook her head no, begging him silently to stop. He was undeterred. "I'll let you have your panties back, if you play nice," he whispered.

Yes! Play nice! her nerve endings shrieked.

Determined to retain some level of composure, she tried to wriggle away. She shifted to the left; he followed. Two inches to the right; he met her there. Then she was pressing against his hand, covering her hot, flushed face with the blanket, stuffing it in her mouth, grinding it between clenched teeth to stop herself from shouting. There was agony as her ears popped, darts of pain shot down her legs as they cramped up, but she wanted more.

His mouth was near her ear. "There you go. You're in. And you know what? Soon as we land, the moment we check into our hotel, we're forming a club of our own." His hand didn't stop moving.

Her mouth was so dry she could barely get the words out. "What club?"

"The Every-Which-Way Club. I get to be president."

Sounded good to her. There was one thing, though; she might have been inducted into the Mile High Club, but he'd missed it by a hair's breadth. "I wish you'd…" She puffed, fighting for air. "I wish you'd made it in with me tonight."

The smile on his face was slow and dangerous. "There's always the flight back," he reminded her.

Chapter 16

Elliot tried to squeeze as much as he could into their first day in Martinique. He forbade Shani from even mentioning their real mission on the island: there'd be time enough for that. He wanted to see her happy, at least for one day.

Their hotel was in Trois-Ilets, to the north of the capital. An intimate cluster of beachside cabins, built out of natural wood and surrounded by thick, lush clusters of bougainvillea, hibiscus, bird-of-paradise and flowers he didn't recognize, and didn't care to know the names of. He just knew they made Shani smile.

Nestled in a colorful woven hammock on the tiny porch, they could rock gently and look out onto the glittering sea. The sea looked as if it was breathing, in and out, like an animal that had been sleeping for millions of years, waking from time to time to stretch itself, gather the shore and everything on it into its arms, then drift into slumber again.

They visited an art gallery, a rum distillery and several bookstores. They had lunch in Fort-de-France in a restaurant that looked two hundred years old. Whitewash flaked from the walls, and ferns poked through cracks. The waitresses wore long, flouncy dresses that would have dazzled him with their whiteness, had they not been partially covered by brilliantly colored madras skirts that reminded him of the way Shani had been dressed the night he met her, in her kente cloth apron and black minidress.

They shopped in Fort-de-France. He bought Shani French perfumes and soaps and, despite her protests, a miniature madras outfit, complete with gold hoop earrings, for Bee. After a dinner of deep green callaloo soup and lobster, they returned to their hotel to make slow, lazy love in the hammock on the porch. No mean feat, that, even for someone as physically fit as he was.

Now, on the morning of day two, the mood was different. When Shani smiled, he knew it was for his benefit. The tension around her mouth almost broke his heart.

"Nice pawpaw," she commented, but she wasn't eating much of it.

"Delicious," he agreed. Everything was delicious: the pawpaw and mango, garnished with mandarin segments and drizzled with bitters and brown sugar, the hot crisp accra—fritters of salted cod—and well-buttered slices of coconut bread. Fruit punch made of watermelon, carambola and tiny bananas no longer than his fingers. He'd have thought he'd died and gone to culinary heaven, if Shani had been enjoying it, too.

He reached across the table for her hand. "It'll be okay," he promised.

She nodded but didn't look convinced.

After breakfast, they took the coastal road, with the sea on their left as they drove to Saint-Pierre. She tried to be a good tour guide and pointed out a few sights, but for the most part she was quiet, looking out the window as the countryside flashed past.

As they entered the northern region, within sight of the Saint-Pierre volcano, the landscape changed. The sea still glittered nearby, never far from view, but gone was the white sand. In its place were shiny black rocks of cooled lava, strewn across the bay like beached seals. The volcano loomed before them, sinister and green, quiet for now.

Trust her pretentious bastard of a husband to have chosen the most dramatic place on the island to establish his lair! Elliot slowed down as they entered the village, taking directions from Shani until he pulled up beside a building which, like so many others nearby, looked as though it had been built directly onto the ruins of a volcanic eruption. New masonry was jammed against old, plaster holding the two disparate materials together. It was a simple two-story building, with the same tinted whitewash he'd seen elsewhere, the kind that left a chalky residue on the fingers and smelled vaguely sweet.

He parked and got out, helping Shani out the other side. Her hand was cold. He squeezed it. "I love you," he told her. "Remember that."

She was trembling, almost imperceptibly. "Elliot, whatever happens…however this turns out…I…" She was trying so hard to breathe, he wished he could breathe for her. "Thank you," she finished lamely. He felt her nails digging into his palm.

The door to the building was modern, with tinted glass, a brass plate displaying Christophe Matthieu's name and a smaller sign that said OUVERT. He shoved the door open and led Shani inside. The studio walls were lined with large, framed paintings, most of them of local views: sunsets, fishing boats, smiling children and other touristy claptrap.

Elliot wasn't impressed. Even if he didn't have a million reasons to hate the guy sight unseen, he'd still think the photos were cheesy and uninspired.

In response to the high-pitched electronic *ding* set off by their arrival, the inner door swung open, and a slender man sauntered in. The first thing that entered Elliot's mind was how much the man's sandy coloring reminded him of Stack. His hair held a crisp wave, and as he lifted his eyes, Elliot was immediately struck by their chilling, flat blue. They were irrefutable evidence of his Metropolitan French ancestry, but somehow they didn't fit his face. The genetic vagary transformed what would have been a reasonably handsome face into something vaguely otherworldly. Those eyes gave Elliot the creeps. Strike one million and one, he thought.

Christophe Matthieu hadn't seen Shani yet, mainly because she'd slipped partially behind Elliot as the door had swung open. The man propped his face into a tourist-welcoming smile, recognizing Elliot off the bat as a foreigner. "May I help you?"

"I'd say you could."

"Would you like to look around? Are you looking for something in particular?"

"I have no intention of looking around, but yeah, you're damn right I'm looking for something in particular."

Matthieu frowned, a little puzzled by Elliot's tone. "Pardon?"

Elliot knew he was being churlish, but he didn't give a damn. The knowledge that he was in the presence of the man who had caused Shani so much humiliation and embarrassment made the hair on the back of his arms stand up. Images of Shani, naked and provocative, swam before his eyes. Photos snapped in a moment that should have remained private, but which this SOB had cast out there like pearls before swine.

"We did come for something," he enunciated carefully, half afraid that he was mad enough to bite the tip of his own tongue, "and we're not leaving before we get it."

Uncertainty flashed in Matthieu's eyes, and his glance flicked from Elliot's face to the counter behind him, where, no doubt, the panic button for the store was concealed. "I keep…not very much money on the premises," he began to stammer.

So he thought it was a robbery. It would have amused Elliot to allow him to wallow in the idea for a few more moments, but right then, Shani chose to slip out from behind him.

"Christophe," she said. Her voice was strong. "I've come for my photos."

The milky blue eyes bugged. "Shani! *Qu'est-ce que tu fais ici?*"

"I just told you—I came to get my photos."

Matthieu floundered and then recovered enough to say, "You mean *my* photos, *sûrement?*"

"They're mine, and you know it."

"I know no such thing," he snapped. He glared at Elliot, all pretense of being pleasant gone. Sizing him up like a dog whose yard had been invaded by a stray. "And who is this, your lawyer? Your Mr. Dorian Black?"

Shani gave Elliot a startled look, as if that idea had never occurred to her. "No, he's not my lawyer." She reached out and laid a hand on Elliot's sleeve, a gesture that was more territorial than reassuring.

Matthieu looked comically confused for several seconds, and then gave a sharp, surprised laugh. "Do not tell me… you cannot wish me to believe that this…person…is a…

lover of some sort? And this, what, a month after we divorce? You work fast, my dear…."

Elliot took a step forward, feeling the acrid vapor of dislike rise in his nostrils like the stench of ammonia. "Listen, brother, we can do this easy, or we can do it hard—"

Shani's arm tightened on his. "I came for my photos. And you're going to give them to me."

Matthieu shrugged with exaggerated French eloquence. "Of course, wife—"

"She's not your wife anymore!"

"Ah, yes. I forget." Matthieu laughed and directed his conversation at Shani once more. "I told you—these photos are yours, in exchange for freedom from your financial demands. I assume you have walked with the relevant documents?"

"She walked with no such thing—" Elliot began.

"Maybe you can tell your new friend to guard his tongue," Matthieu suggested.

"Maybe we could step outside, and then you can repeat that," Elliot shot back. His loathing of this man was growing by the second, but a workout on the sidewalk would help him vent some of it.

Shani lifted her hand, dampening his bloody fantasy by saying firmly, "Elliot, I can handle this."

Elliot swallowed hard, biting back his anger for her sake. Love stayed his hand. *This is her battle,* he reminded himself. *Let her fight it. And pretty please, Jesus, let her win.*

"I have no documents," Shani said. "I came to you as the mother of your child, to appeal to your reason. You don't love me anymore…" Pain flickered across her face. "I don't know if you ever did…." She waited for him to say something, to confirm or deny. Elliot waited too, feeling as if something inside him were dying.

The flat blue eyes showed no reaction.

"But Bee's your daughter. You must love her."

"I am very much concerned for her welfare," he said, as though that were the same thing.

"Well, then, for her sake, please, give me back those photos. Is this the way you want her to know her mother? Revealed and naked to the eyes of the world? You want her growing up hearing the whispers, hearing people call me a slut?"

"This is a matter for adults, not for children. This doesn't have to reach her world…."

"But our world *is* her world. Kids aren't protected from grown-up things like they were before. If you put those photos out there, don't you think it's just a matter of time before someone sees them and recognizes me? A parent at her day care. Someone at the grocery store. She'll see the stares and hear the whispers. She won't understand what they're about, but she'll know something's wrong." Shani stepped closer to Matthieu, hands out and open, and everything in Elliot screamed for her to step back, get away.

"You say this publisher has a website? The internet is forever. Those photos will still be there in ten years. I don't want her to see them, or hear about them, and hate me." She swallowed hard. A thin line of sweat formed on her upper lip. Elliot wanted to wipe it away with his thumb.

"I'm appealing to your fatherhood," she persisted. "I'm appealing to your manhood…."

Matthieu looked trapped by her logic, by the sincerity of her appeal. He knew he was losing ground, and he fought for a way to regain it. He chose the moral low ground.

"Ah, yes, I remember how much you used to yearn for my *manhood*...."

"You know that's not what I meant!"

Matthieu smiled nervously, uncomfortable now that Shani had put him in such a position, using his daughter as leverage. "I understand what you say."

"Good." Her relief was palpable.

"But the financial matter, this is still a problem."

Shani groaned. "Bee deserves the money, Christophe—"

"Béatrice!" Matthieu snapped. "This is the girl's name! Use it!"

"She's my daughter too, and I'll call her what I damn... well...please!" Shani punctuated the last three words with a pounding fist, coming down hard on the counter beside her. Her face was hot, and her eyes glowed like those of a mother bear whose offspring had been threatened.

Elliot couldn't stop staring. This is the woman who was so afraid of meeting this creep that she couldn't even swallow her breakfast? Who'd hidden behind him like a kindergartener when they'd walked in?

"My daughter is entitled to a college fund, and decent health care. She deserves toys and birthday parties, and vacations and pretty clothes. You took away my ability to pay for these things with your spitefulness. But I will not let you shortchange her. You'll keep on making her payments, if I have to drag you into court again. If I have to get a lien on your shop—"

Matthieu looked around in horror.

"Those payments are non-negotiable," Shani ground out. "Don't test me."

"And your alimony?"

"You know what?" She made a gesture as if she were throwing the money at him, so violently that he flinched.

"I don't need it. I'm going to get my job back. I'm done waitressing, and I'm done living on a shoestring. I lived well before I met you, and I sure as hell can live well now. Keep the damn alimony...."

Good for you, sweetheart, Elliot thought.

Matthieu brightened. "So, you are willing to negotiate?"

"Yes!" Shani said wearily. "Give me the photos, and we'll call it a deal. Keep up Bee's payments, and you can forget mine."

Elliot watched Matthieu work it over in his mind. He set his feet apart and folded his arms, trying to look as thuggish as possible. Shani had done a good job on her own, but a little intimidation never hurt.

"I will get this in writing, yes?"

"I'll talk to Dorian as soon as I get back."

Matthieu knew a good deal when he saw it. "Wait here. I will bring the disk." He threw a hard blue glare at Elliot. "Don't touch anything."

"I wouldn't dream of it."

While Matthieu was gone, Elliot and Shani stood silent in the little studio, separated by several feet. There were a dozen things he wanted to tell her, but there was something about the way she held her body, the harsh rise and fall of her breasts, that told him to hold his tongue. Which was fine by him; he felt almost too sick to speak.

He'd been around; he'd met dirtbags of every stripe. But this guy, he was different. Arrogant, mean-spirited and cruel, he made the blood in Elliot's veins chill and the bile in his throat rise. And yet Shani had loved him. How? Why?

He was catapulted back to the first day he and Shani had made love, in her dinky little bedroom with the kiddie sheets on the bed, when she'd held out on him—for love of this man. When she'd regaled him with more information than he'd needed about just how good this jerk had been in bed. He thought again about the photos of her, and how willing she'd been to let this man take them. There'd been a look in her eye, the look of a woman just gliding back down to earth after having taken flight on the wings of an orgasm. The knowledge that that look had been put there by this creep made him giddy.

His stomach rolled again. He put his hand to it, urging it to settle.

Shani spotted the gesture. "You okay?"

He nodded wordlessly, but his mind was doing somersaults. Shani had made love to this man, and borne his child. She'd loved him. If Matthieu was an example of her taste in men, what did that say about him? He felt the genesis of a headache at the base of his skull, and he knew it was going to be a beast of a migraine once it was fully grown.

Matthieu returned with a small black memory card in his hand. He made sure to keep the counter between them as a barrier, and he held the card out to Shani. She hesitated and then took it. Elliot could see the merest tremble of her fingers.

"This is the only copy?" she asked.

Matthieu raised a brow. "You do not trust me?"

She shook her head wordlessly.

"Yet I trust you to keep your end of the bargain." He tut-tutted elaborately. "I imagine, as I trust you, you must trust me." The thin lips pulled back. "That card is the master. I assure you, my dear, that it is all there is." The icy laser of his eyes was on Elliot. "I do very good work, my friend. You might enjoy looking at them."

Not as much as I'd enjoy scraping you off the bottom of my shoe, Elliot thought.

"And you will have your Mr. Black call my lawyer, yes? To ensure that this question of alimony is behind us?"

She nodded. "And Bee?"

"*Béatrice* will be well taken care of. You have my word as a gentleman." The irony of the statement seemed to escape him.

Shani stared down at the card, turning it over and over, as if asking herself how this small, innocuous-looking object could have posed such a threat. Elliot had had enough of standing aside and letting her handle it. He crossed the space between them and slipped his arm around her waist. "C'mon, baby. We have what we need. Let's go."

"'Kay." Mesmerized by the shiny object in her hand, she didn't move.

"I'll be seeing you," Matthieu promised, "when I come to visit my daughter." He bared his teeth at Elliot and held out his hand. "And I suppose I owe you my thanks, *mec*."

Elliot frowned at the hand, not taking it. "Why's that?"

"Why? You've relieved me of a burden, of course."

Elliot could smell smoke curling up from under his collar. Every atom within him screeched danger, but he couldn't stop himself from asking, "What burden is that?"

"Ah, the tedious burden of servicing my perpetually horny ex-wife every time I visit the States to see my child—"

Matthieu was light; Elliot was able to drag him over the counter with just one hand. With a twist of Elliot's wrist, the polo collar around the man's neck grew tight, and the watery eyes bulged.

"Elliot!" Shani screamed.

Elliot barely heard her over the roar of bloody rage in his

ears. He shook Matthieu off as if detaching a Chihuahua latched onto his forearm, sending him skating into a row of framed photos. They clattered to the floor: uninspired shots of grinning fishermen, slightly lewd wide-angle shots of banana trees laden with their phallic fruit. As Matthieu struggled to find his feet, he stepped on a frame, and the sound of breaking glass split the air.

Elliot closed in, his vision narrowing fast, his rage a fever. The coward didn't have it in him to raise his hands, even to pretend to fight back. Elliot's fist closed over Matthieu's collar and he dragged him to his feet. "Inside or outside—I don't care."

"Shani! Tell this lunatic to stop!"

As much as Elliot knew she was there, feet from him, he couldn't even see her. Flame-hot brimstone rained in his head. Mount Pelée erupting, bringing only devastation. He didn't know how it happened, but Matthieu was airborne, and then on his back on the counter, sniveling. Elliot loomed over him, one hand pressing down on his chest. "Don't you ever speak about my woman like that!" His voice was a pit-bull growl, coming from deep in his gut. "I swear to you—!"

"Shani, please!" Matthieu begged.

"Stop!" Shani's arms were around his waist in a desperate embrace. She was sobbing. "Elliot, Elliot…!" was all she could say.

"Stay out of this," he warned.

"I will not stay out of this," she shrilled. "I'm telling you to stop!"

Elliot struggled to harness the crazy firestorm. Through a curtain of red, he had a vision of his immediate future: Matthieu bleeding with the imprint of his fist blossoming on that high-bridged nose, Elliot feeling a whole lot better.

But the woman he loved was pleading with him to spare this ox. For her sake, and only hers…

He turned his head in her direction, to tell her she'd prevailed over his baser instincts, but as he did so, Matthieu's arm snaked out and grabbed a small framed photo, and the next thing Elliot was aware of was a shower of sparks behind his eyes as the glass shattered against his jaw. It was like landing face-first into a box of razors, a pain that was almost exquisite.

He staggered in disbelief, letting the jerk go and putting his hand to his face. It came away striped with red.

Matthieu was smirking, pleased with his petty victory. "Fool. You waste your time. Fighting over a little whore who has nothing to offer you except my leftovers—"

Elliot's fist in his mouth made it impossible to finish the utterance. The man landed on the ground like a sack of garbage. Elliot dropped to his knees, but not to pray. He could feel the soft, pampered flesh give under his knuckles as he pounded. Air escaped from the man's parted lips in a grunt as each bow landed.

And each blow bought a little redemption for Shani. *This* is for the first set of photos, Elliot thought. And *this* is for the second. *This* is for what you just called my woman, and *this* is for her daughter…

He felt the solidity of Shani's warm body at his back. He heard her beg him to stop. She yanked at him, arms clasped around him, an ant desperately trying to shift a mountain. When she realized he was too heavy and too powerful for her to move by force, she rested her head against his back, crying into the fabric of his shirt.

Just one more punch, he thought. One more. For *me*. But he could feel the tears soaking into the back of his shirt, and they dampened his rage like droplets of rain from heaven, quenching the fires of hell. He let up on Matthieu and stepped back.

"She's the one who saved you," he snarled. "Remember that." His face hurt. He could feel blood trickle into his collar. He wondered if there were shards embedded in his cheek. He touched it gingerly.

He looked to Shani, desperately needing to hold her. Knowing that her touch would make things better. For a second, he was jerked backward through time, found himself a teenager again, sore and aching, but knowing that his mother's touch would make things better. But her touch would never come.

Neither would Shani's. With a gasp, she tore her arms from around him and darted toward her ex-husband, sinking before him. Matthieu struggled to get up, wiping his mouth. His skin was a sickening gray, like a corpse washed up on the beach.

"Are you okay?" Shani asked.

Elliot was incredulous. Was *Matthieu* okay?

"Get out," the man snarled as he shook her off, "before I call the *gendarmes*." He had recovered enough to haul himself to his feet. He wiped his mouth on his sleeve.

Getting out seemed like a good idea—for more reasons than one. The nausea that had set in the moment he entered the room was about to get the better of him. Shani was wiping her palms on the front of her jeans, not Elliot's blood, wiped away by her tender hands, but the blood of the enemy, which he'd drawn for her.

It made him sick.

He walked to the door and yanked it open. Sunlight stabbed at him. He stood on the sidewalk outside the shop, hands on his hips, wondering what to do next. The creak of the door told him she'd followed him out.

She was at his elbow. "It's over." She touched him

slightly on the arm. She came around to look up at him, her face full of concern.

Now she was concerned? He flinched and moved away. Hurt and puzzlement crossed her face, but she didn't try to touch him again. Instead, she walked meekly to the car and stood at the door, waiting for him.

He walked on by. With the thunder still pounding between his ears, a car in his hands would be a weapon. He needed some time to bring his passions under control. Besides, he and Shani needed to thrash something out.

Now.

Chapter 17

Elliot stomped along the road until he came upon a flight of stone steps leading down to the beach. The sun was high, beating down on him, not doing his headache a favor. The sea below was dark because of the volcanic sand; it held a threatening kind of beauty, a somber and dangerous place framed by the brilliant glory of the sky and the rampaging flowers that grew everywhere.

But he was sick to death of the beauty, sick of the sunshine and the colors. He was sick of the island, which just went nonchalantly on, serene and splendid, not caring whether he was happy, sad or mad enough to bite the head off a bat. He longed for darkness, even for the cold of a Santa Amata fall. Why should everything on the outside be so glorious when everything on the inside of him was so many jarring shades of gray?

He thudded down the stairs, hearing the clack of Shani's sandals behind him. The round, hard volcanic pebbles on the beach were a far cry from the powdery white sand closer to the city, but he enjoyed the pressure of it, pushing back under his shoes. It crunched as he walked.

"Elliot!" Shani struggled to keep up. "Honey, please!"

He heard her footsteps, desperate and quick. He could have kept on at his pace, longed to, but he slowed down a little lest she trip and fall face-first onto the rocks.

She caught up with him, hand grasping his upper arm, like a drowning woman reaching for a buoy. "Wait up," she puffed.

"Keep up."

"No." With surprising strength, she held on to his arm with both hands. Stones ground under her feet as she dug in. "You're stopping, and you're talking to me."

He spun to face her. "I've stopped," he informed her unnecessarily.

She struggled for breath. "Why are you so mad?"

"You don't know?"

"He was just trying to needle you."

"He did a damn fine job."

She went on. "You know, get your goat. It's a man thing. Territory."

"A man thing," he repeated slowly. If he hadn't been so furious, he'd have found it funny. *She* was lecturing to *him* about man stuff? "And...?"

She looked puzzled. "And what?"

"Is it true?" She still didn't look as if she got him, so he clarified. "Did you sleep with him?"

"Who?"

"Tupac! Geez, Shani, are you trying to be difficult? Did you sleep with Matthieu? It's a simple question. It's got a yes-or-no answer."

She blinked, incredulous. "He was my husband."

"I meant *after* you filed for divorce!"

She finally got his meaning, and her face flushed. The red flood of shame under her dark skin made her even more beautiful. "That's none of your business."

"I love you. That makes it my business."

"It was before I met you!"

"How long before you met me?"

"Does it matter?"

"It does to me!"

"Why?"

He couldn't believe she was asking that. Why? The idea of Shani letting this pig touch her, and enjoying it, almost made his lungs cease to function. "I can't stand the thought of this man's hands on you. Him being inside of you." He shuddered.

"That was then. This is now. It's never going to happen again. He'll turn up twice, maybe three times a year, spend half a day with Bee, and then leave. You never have to see him. And other than that, I won't have to see him, either. It's over."

"How can I be so sure?"

Her lips thinned. "You're just going to have to take my word for it."

He stared down at the pebbles between his feet, wanting to wing them, one by one, into the rolling sea, until the beach was a void. A heavy sigh shuddered out of him.

"You knew I wasn't a virgin," she said quietly. "Just as I knew you weren't."

"Yeah," he threw at her. "But at least the people *I've* slept with don't have horns and a tail!" Grow up, a voice inside his head told him, but he refused to listen.

"You can't wish away something that's already happened," she pleaded. "I was alone and lonely. I had no one, for a long time, and he was just…there." She paused, and the pain on her face made his heart crack. "I never meant to hurt you."

She was speaking of hurt. The real truth, the *real* source of his hurt, tumbled from his lips. "You went to him."

"I…?"

The blood on his cheek was beginning to get sticky. He longed to wipe it away, but he left it there, a physical manifestation of his emotional wound. "We were both hurt, but you ran to *him*." The buzzing in his head grew louder, and the image of Shani before him flickered, was replaced by his mother and then flickered back.

"I was afraid you'd hurt him bad enough to get you in trouble. He was going to call the cops."

She was making sense. He hated that she was, because it forced him to be rational, and right now, he didn't want to. He knew he was being infantile, but abandonment and loss washed him away, just like when his mother left him for good. It was as if the tide had suddenly come in with a vengeance, swamping him. "You made a choice, and it wasn't me."

"I did make a choice. I'm standing before you."

He felt as tired as death. "Well, then, you made it too late."

"Elliot, you're wrong. Don't do this…." The tears Shani had shed for her husband had left dirty tracks on her cheeks. She wasn't shedding any more now, but the emptiness of her eyes scared him even more. She put her hand to her neck and rolled her head, a gesture he was familiar with. It made his heart ache. He could stop this now, take her into his arms, but his head was pounding too hard.

They were balanced, fragile, in a bubble of nontime, where everything would stand still, no decisions made, until someone opened their mouth. Until then, everything could be saved. Until then, all was lost.

"What about Bee?" she asked. "She adores you."

"I love her."

"Then we don't need to do this. We can move on and be in love and be happy. The three of us."

Everything in him wanted to agree with her. In his soul, he knew she was right. But hurt and betrayal had created a gulf he couldn't cross. So he stayed on his side, staring across the emptiness, unable to speak. "I'm so...tired," he groaned eventually, but not necessarily to her. "I need to rest."

She gestured toward the stairs in the distance. "Then let's go back."

Go with her, a voice said. But he shook his head. It hurt so much he could barely see. It was as if all the air had been sucked out of the sky, and the black sand was jerked from under him. He was standing, suspended, at the epicenter of nowhere.

"Is this over?" he heard her ask.

"I don't know."

She held out her hand. For a second, he thought she wanted to shake, like strangers. But she was holding out the memory card. "Take it."

He frowned at it as if it were a doomsday device. "I don't..."

She thrust it at him. "Please, Elliot. Get rid of it. I can't bear to look at it." She hesitated. "Thank you...for what you did. And I'm sorry I disappointed you." Then gravel crunched as she walked away.

I disappointed myself, he wanted to tell her, but by then she was too far away to hear. Sunlight danced along the holographic label of the card, breaking up into a rainbow of colors. Elliot knelt and ran his fingers through the rough sand, searching. The black stones were, for the most part, small, smooth and round, worn away by time and tide, but he found one that would do the job. Vengefully, he smashed the small plastic square, obliterating its data for good. He considered flinging it into the sea, but instead shoved it into his pocket.

When he looked up, Shani had disappeared from view. He wanted to race after her as if he was being carried on the wind, but his body betrayed him.

Elliot would never quite be able to understand the phenomenon, but the rest of the afternoon drained away at a pace that left him disoriented. People lurched jerkily past at an unnatural speed, like something out of a Charlie Chaplin movie: children out for a swim, fishermen bringing in their boats, joggers thumping by. Clouds raced across the sky, and the sun fell to the horizon as if someone had dunked a basketball. But the heat persisted relentlessly.

Elliot sat at the foot of the steps, not trusting his legs to get him to the top. His headache was like a living, malignant presence; to turn his head was to bring flashing silver shards of pain slicing through his skull. He sat there with his head in his hands, counting breaths.

He finally dragged himself back to street level, staggered to his car and fumbled with his keys. Steady, he told himself. Careful. Keep within the speed limit, and keep your eyes on the road. You'll make it back.

The hotel cabin was empty when he got there; Shani's things were gone from the closet. This didn't surprise him. If he were to be honest with himself, he'd delayed his return either consciously or unconsciously for just that reason: to give her time to leave with dignity. The envelope from the travel agency sat on the dresser. Her ticket was missing.

Their flight was scheduled for the next afternoon, but he didn't have the strength—or the guts—to get on the phone just as she had and change his booking, giving him half a chance of catching up to her. Instead he flipped the lights off, flopped down onto the bed with his shoes still on and slept through the night as if he'd been drugged.

Chapter 18

"I. Am. Not. A. Bee!"

Shani watched in puzzled frustration as her daughter threw herself onto the rug and wailed. Her two afro-puffs bobbed in rhythm as she kicked her heels, slamming them down onto the floor as she yelled. Puddin' thought it was a game and pounced on Bee's fat little tummy with a *rowr!* of delight.

Not a bee? This was the kid who hardly wore anything that wasn't black and yellow, who had every bee-related toy that ever buzzed out of a factory and who drizzled honey on everything, including eggs? *This* child was turning her back on beedom?

Shani stooped down, holding out the bee-striped pajamas she'd bought. "But they're your favorites, sweetheart." She held them up so Bee could see the embroidery on the front. "Look—there's Winnie the Pooh, and Eeyore, and a big pot of honey, and a bee. No, two bees! You love bees, don't you?"

Bee pouted. "Nope."

"But I got this just for you…"

"I don't care, and I hate it, and I'm not a baby anymore and I don't like Winnie the Pooh and I'm not a bee."

The parent's manual had said there'd be days like this. Shani inhaled slowly and asked, "Okay, sweetie. What are you, then?"

"I'm a fairy princess!"

Easy enough, Shani thought. I can live with that. "Are you? And what made you decide you're a fairy princess?"

Bee sat up with a big grin, tantrum over. "Elliot says I am."

The mention of the name sent sharp prickles along Shani's spine. Elliot. Jeez. She tried to school her features into something that was at least neutral, even if she couldn't manage pleasant. Just because she wanted three minutes in the ring with the man didn't mean it was fair to shake Bee's unswerving devotion to him. She kept her tone casual. "Did he?"

Bee nodded, brightening at the chance to wax lyrical about her hero. "He says I'm his pretty little princess and he'll get me a white *oo*-nicorn and it'll have big pink wings and a horn and can fly through rainbows and I don't like bees anymore so I don't want your stinky old pajamas. I want princess pajamas so when Elliot comes with my oo-nicorn I'll be ready."

Great. First a kitten, now a unicorn. Positive visualization was a good thing: it helped soothe the nerves. Shani visualized herself positively whacking Elliot about the head with the box the Winnie the Pooh pajamas came in. "Okay, honey…"

"I don't like honey anymore, either. Princesses eat fairy cake and ice cream…"

She sighed. "Right, my little fairy. I'll get you some new pajamas in the morning, okay?"

"'Kay." Bee threw a wide grin at Gina, who had been standing by, gravely watching the scenario. "Mama's gonna get me some fairy princess pajamas, Gina!"

"That's lovely, Bee," Gina cooed.

Deciding it wouldn't be a bad idea to be alone for a few minutes, Shani suggested, "Gina, how about you take Bee into the living room? You can watch her princess DVDs while I fix dinner."

Bee squealed, "Fair-y prin-cess! Fair-y prin-cess!" and danced out to the living room. The kitten danced out with her, tripping between Bee's feet. Gina didn't move a muscle. Instead, she called after Bee, "I'll catch up with you, princess!"

Shani couldn't keep the surprise off her face, as the teenager folded her arms across her chest and rested her skinny butt against the kitchen counter. First the little kid had decided to abruptly change species, and now the big kid was disobeying a direct order. Was anything sane in the world anymore? She folded her arms in echo and asked, "What is it, Gina?"

Gina cut to the chase. "Where's Elliot?"

Shani liked Gina; the Paks were the closest thing she had to family, but the kid was out of line. She answered gently, "I don't think you should be asking me that."

Silken black brows drew together. "Why not?"

"Because what happened between Elliot and me is just that—between Elliot and me."

"No, it's not. Bee's here, too. She loves him." Gina gave her a direct look, too young yet to learn how to pull her punches. "You love him."

You're kind of hung up on him yourself, Shani thought, but she closed her eyes so the hurt wouldn't show. Oh, for the days when Gina's chagrin over her *last* tiff with Elliot had manifested itself in silence! "Gina," she began, "you're just a kid..."

"I'm seventeen," Gina reminded her, sticking out her puny chest inside the oversize Little Brother T-shirt that had been a gift from Elliot.

"Doesn't make you a grown-up."

Gina snorted. "Look who's talking about being a grown-up! The two of you are driving me crazy. One minute you're all over each other, the next minute you're not talking, then you're off to Martinique for some sort of honeymoon—"

"That was business," Shani interrupted, but the memory of the sexual feast they'd found there, even before the plane touched down, made her face go hot.

"Right." Gina nodded. Her pretty red mouth twisted in disbelief. "Next thing we know, you're back a day early and your eyes are red. And he hasn't been by in a week. So, what happened?"

What happened was that I screwed up. I hit Elliot where it hurt the most, and then...things fell apart. She frowned and turned away. "People break up."

"And people get back together."

"I don't need relationship advice from a kid," Shani snapped.

"You're gonna get it," Gina answered. She looked the same as her mother when she was chastising rowdy customers, her pale skin lit up from within, her eyes filled with dragon fire. "Elliot's one of the good guys. There aren't a lot of them around. And he's a whole lot better than that...dude...who used to turn up here."

"That *dude* was my husband," Shani reminded her tautly.

"Ex," Gina emphasized. "And he looked like a creep."

Shani really didn't need this. She hadn't had a good night's sleep since Martinique. And now, to be lectured… She rubbed her head. "Gina, I like you a whole lot…"

Gina ignored her. "He loves you! You can see it every time he looks at you. And he loves Bee. You know how many guys out there his age wanna take on a woman who has a kid? Puh-leeze!"

She hated it when people made sense. Especially people half her age. "The thing with Elliot's…well…it's complicated."

"Ain't it always?"

Shani frowned at her feet.

"Whyn't you call him?"

"I doubt he's in a mood to take my calls."

"Then go over and see him."

"Like that'd make it better."

"Go over there with your coat on, and nuthin' underneath."

"Gina!"

Gina pouted prettily, tauntingly. "I'm not as young as you think." The pout spread into a grin. "Or my folks think."

A lecture on her relationship was bad enough, but an exposé on teenage sexuality was a little beyond her level of endurance. She tried to sound stern. "Bee's all alone right now."

Gina tilted to one side so she could see out into the living room, and then righted herself. "She's safe. She's watching Elliot's princess DVD."

Kid couldn't take a hint. "What I meant was…"

Gina rolled her eyes. "Whatcha gonna do? Fire me?"

"You know I'd never do that." Shani couldn't hold back a smile.

Gina smiled back. "Then trust me. Elliot's a good guy. I don't know what's got you two pissed off at each other *again*, but it's nothing you can't fix. Just don't let him go." She walked across the kitchen floor and put her small hand over Shani's as she passed. Her nails were a ghastly combination of pearl white and sparkly purple, the same shade as the fresh streaks in her hair. "You'll get over it," she said, gave her a wide, naive smile, and sauntered off to be with Bee.

Shani wasn't so sure.

"Elliot!" Stack's secretary, Mrs. Oliphant, hopped to her feet as Elliot stalked past. "Your father's in a meeting!" She stepped in front of him, her small frame hardly a deterrent.

He looked down at her. As always, she was precisely dressed, although a little less cool and unflustered than usual, which wasn't surprising, given that Elliot had stormed in unannounced looking as if he'd spent the night on the streets. His jeans were so grubby they could have walked out the door on their own.

"You look like you slept in a storm drain. And you smell bad."

He'd known Mrs. Oliphant since his teens; she was like a fussy, well-meaning aunt. He took no offense. He agreed almost unconcernedly. "I know."

The deep gray eyes examined him carefully. "What's that on your neck? Did you get cut? You okay?"

The wounds Christophe had inflicted on him were healing. He touched them lightly. "No. But I will be, once I get in there."

Mrs. Oliphant looked anxious. "You two been fighting again?"

"Not yet."

She searched his face. "Sure you don't want to…maybe cool down first? I'm sure whatever's bothering you…"

"Don't think I can cool down, Mrs. O. I've been trying for a week and…" It didn't make sense, standing here arguing. What he needed was on the other side of that door. He took one step forward.

She backed up a little and then stood her ground. "I'm sorry, but he really is in a—"

"Meeting, I know."

She spun her wedding ring around on her finger, once, twice. "Why don't you have a seat until his guests come out? They won't be long."

Sit? Wait? While this fire burned inside, after a week of stoking it, feeding it with years of hurt and resentment? Even if he was willing to try—and he wasn't—he'd probably explode. He shook his head. "Sorry. I have to see him. Now."

Mrs. Oliphant looked about to protest again, but something in his eyes stopped her. She threw one anxious glance at Stack's door and sighed. She stepped aside.

He gave her a half smile. "If he asks, I'll tell him you were in the ladies' room when I got here."

She nodded gratefully and hurried back to her desk.

Stack was sitting in his lounge area, in one of the plush chairs. His deep charcoal suit didn't show a wrinkle, even though he had one ankle casually resting on his knee, and his long arm was draped along the back of the chair. He held a glass of amber liquid in one hand.

Stack's two guests turned toward the sound of the door. The exotic copper glow of their skin and the sharpness of their angular features suggested they were East African.

They were seated just as comfortably as Stack was, also holding drinks. If there was one thing Stack knew how to do, it was to lull his business contacts into a sense of complacency, plying them with good liquor and regaling them with his wit and charm as he positioned them for the kill. Elliot wondered almost distractedly if they had any clue who they were dealing with.

Stack smiled, giving Elliot the impression he was actually glad to see him, but his eyes were ringed with uncertainty. "Elliot! Haven't heard from you in, what, a week? Been out of town?"

"Something like that."

The two foreigners were on their feet, so Stack rose, too. "Gentlemen, this is my son, Elliot Bookman Jr. Elliot, these are Mr. Nagenda and Mr. Quaraishy. We were discussing some business…" He eyed Elliot warily. "We should be done soon, if you'd like to wait in the lobby…."

Elliot shook hands with the men and returned their grave little bows equally gravely, but he made no move to leave.

"Elliot…?"

"I need to speak to you."

The idea that something was seriously wrong seemed to gel in Stack's mind, because his lips became a thin line. "I'll be with you in a few minutes." He nodded in the direction of the door.

The visitors were equally sensitive to the undercurrents coursing through the room—how could they not be? Tension made the rafters vibrate. They set their glasses down and held out their hands. "Mr. Bookman," the older one said, "we will take our leave. It has been a pleasure. We can speak again in the morning."

Stack protested. "But—"

"We hope the rest of your afternoon is pleasant," he said,

but the assessing look he gave Elliot said he very much doubted it.

Stack had no choice but to accede, and he walked them to the door with as much grace as he could muster, shaking their hands once more as they left before carefully sliding the lock into place and returning to the sitting area. His face was stone. He knocked his drink back, slamming the glass down on the table. "That was business. It was important."

"I'm sorry." Elliot was surprised to find he really was. Rudeness wasn't one of his weaknesses. "But so's this." The weight that had bogged down his soul for so long had come between him and Shani, and he knew that if he could get rid of it, he could go to her a free man. And the time had come.

Stack shrugged and swung his eyes in the direction of his minibar. "Drink?"

Elliot shook his head. "Not that thirsty."

"Mind if I do?"

"I do mind, actually. Whyn't you sit through this one sober?"

"You accusing me of being a drunk?"

"Not at this very moment."

Stack stood just feet from him, searching his eyes. Elliot lifted his jaw and suffered the scrutiny, even though it made his skin burn. He was clamping down so hard his teeth hurt. Stack exhaled through his nose. "Okay. Spit it."

Spit it. After a week's torment, in which he'd gone through a dozen fevered, imaginary conversations, he was face-to-face with his father, and he didn't know what to say. He'd fantasized walking in and unleashing a firestorm; he'd revised and rehearsed every thing he was going to say, honed every weapon he was going to hurl.

And now he was here, and instead of spewing poison, he was almost mute.

He looked around the office but saw none of the decor, not even the butt-ugly paintings that always assaulted his eyes. Instead, he saw the office through the eyes of his teenage self.

Back then, his father had been sleeping with his mother's sister; Elliot had yelled at him, cursed at him, pleaded with him to stop. Stack had been cool, unashamed and dismissive, suggesting he was a kid yet and should keep his nose out of the affairs of men. So Elliot had punched him, sending him to the floor. And that gut-tearing encounter had been the nail in the coffin of their father-son relationship.

He tried to suck some air in, but it hurt to breathe.

"Elliot?" Stack's voice came from far off, from across a river of time. "Son?"

He spoke past the acrid knot in his throat. "For fifteen years, you've acted like nothing was wrong. You just went on with your life. Like she wasn't even gone."

Stack squinted, puzzled. Still not getting it.

Time swirled around Elliot, snatching at him and making him dizzy. Loss and grief threatened to swallow him whole. And at the center of that loss, no, the genesis of it, was his father. When the time spiral stopped, he was fourteen again. "You took her from me," he said dully. "I loved her with everything I had in me. And she loved me just the same. She loved you…and you didn't care. You threw it all away!"

From through the mist, he heard his father's voice. "What're you…who…?"

"You chased her away." The pain of it made him almost blind.

Stack's puzzled frown deepened into concern. "Oh. Your mom."

"Yes, my mom! Why didn't you just put your hands around her throat and squeeze? It would've been faster."

"It wasn't my fault."

"How could it *not* be your fault? She killed herself… over you."

"There's no proof of that."

"Proof's inside you, ringing out, if only you had the guts to listen."

Stack sighed again and then gestured at the couch. "Want to sit?"

"No."

"Fine." He stood within inches of Elliot, and Elliot surprised himself by not leaping back to put some space between them. "I need you to hear me."

He tried to focus his eyes on the face that was so like his, and yet so different. He tried to listen.

"Okay," Stack began. "Things weren't going so well between your mother and me when she died."

"You don't say."

"I made a lot of mistakes. I hurt her."

Now that he was hearing the words he'd yearned for all these years, he didn't know how to answer.

Stack filled the void. "I loved her too, you know. I miss her every day."

"You've got a fine way of showing it. You sleep with any woman who's willing, and you drink like a damn fish…."

"Did it ever occur to you that the reason I drink so much is that I miss her?"

"Did it ever occur to you that if you stopped drinking you probably wouldn't act like such a dick all the time? And maybe you could quiet your thoughts long enough to admit to the role you played in her death, and seek forgiveness."

"I *have* asked for forgiveness!"

"Of whom?"

"Of Janice. Of God."

"Well, you never asked me!" To his horror, Elliot realized his vision had blurred completely, filled with tears for the first time since his mother's funeral. That they should fall here, with his father as witness, was bitterer than the tears themselves. He scrubbed them away.

He felt his father's hard arms around him. He hadn't been held like that since he was a boy; it was disconcertingly odd, yet strangely comforting. "Don't touch me," he protested, but he didn't shake Stack off.

He heard his father's voice in his ear. "Son, I'm sorry. Forgive me."

Forgive him? That was asking so much! "I can't."

"I need you to."

"I don't know how."

"It'll come to you." Stack released him, sensing he wouldn't put up with the contact much longer. "Take your time. Just promise me you'll try."

"Everything I've ever done in my life," Elliot said, "every relationship I've ever had…has been tainted. Every woman I've ever wanted to love, only ever got a half portion, because of what happened with Mom. I think I love a woman, and then I get scared. I think she'll leave, just like Mom…."

Stack caught on fast. "What about Shani?"

"What *about* Shani?"

"Are you two…did you break up with her?"

The taut, corded knots of muscle between his shoulders were like coils of tangled rope. The effort it took to shrug was colossal. "I don't know."

"You don't *know*?"

"I'm not sure if I did…it happened so fast. I was so mad, and so sick…"

"About what?"

"Doesn't matter. It was stupid." He still had problems piecing together what had happened on the beach. Whenever he tried, his mind clouded over. "I needed some time to think…."

"I hope not. I like her," Stack said without any hint of irony.

"Huh." Elliot focused on one of the crazy-monkey paintings, glad for something to look at, rather than into his father's discerning eyes. "Wonder if she likes *me*…."

Stack stepped over to the bar, picked up a bottle of Scotch, hesitated and then put it back down again. He popped open a can of soda and split it between two glasses, and came back and handed one over. Elliot took it, surprised at how dehydrated he was.

Stack sipped the drink and grimaced, as if the taste of unadulterated soda was foreign to him. "You know, for such a brilliant man, you really are a damn fool."

"'Scuse me?"

"How could you wonder if she likes you? This woman's had to work hard all her life, had a couple of bad breaks along the way—" He stopped as if afraid he had said too much.

"The photos," Elliot supplied dully.

"She told you."

"Yeah, she told me." Bile rose when he remembered that his father had seen them, but he fought it down.

Stack continued. "This woman has worked all her life, putting up with buttheads like me just to earn a living and take care of her kid. She's willing to make space in her life for you, and take a risk again so soon after getting crapped on by the last man she let into her life. And you wonder if she *likes* you?"

Elliot had a vision of Shani on the beach, pleading for their love, and he was filled with shame.

Stack went on with the determination and confidence of a businessman sealing a deal. "I think it's more than just 'like.' This woman's fallen for you hard, and, if you ask me, you two deserve to be together. Question is, what're you going to do about it?"

Chapter 19

Shani balanced a large cake in both hands, trying to navigate her way across the lawn, avoiding the swarm of children weaving in and out and around her like a school of fish. The thing had an inch of pink frosting, with an airbrushed pattern of a fairy princess riding a white unicorn. It would be a pity to have it fall.

She made it to the picnic table relatively unscathed, with just a smidgen of icing rubbed off on her elbow, narrowly averting a minor catastrophe as she ducked to avoid an airborne Nerf ball.

"Great party," Gina said for about the tenth time that afternoon as she set four pink candles in a row above the unicorn's head. "There's so much space in your yard for the kids to run around in."

Shani glanced around happily. She'd moved into her new house only a few weeks ago, and there was work to be done, but the birthday party was doubling as a celebration of her new life. Pride be damned, gossip be damned, she'd sought and found a new job teaching college history again. She was working on getting her old life back, and it felt wonderful.

"Great party," Shani echoed with a grin. "If you truly enjoy having twenty three- and four-year-olds cranked up on soda and candy zooming around. Is that a cupcake fight going on by the rosebushes?"

"Uh-huh." Gina agreed, but she wasn't focused on Shani at all. Her eyes kept shifting to the front gate.

Shani frowned. Gina seemed even more wired than Bee's classmates. She'd been nervous, distracted and excited all afternoon. Even her blue-streaked hair looked electrified. The clown Shani had hired to work the party had done a cute face-painting job on Gina: her face was a field of lilies, and pink and lavender eye shadow radiated in scrolls toward her hairline. She looked like an anime heroine ready for battle, except the warrior prince hadn't yet rode in on his winged beetle, or whatever it was warrior princes were riding on these days.

Something in Shani tingled. "Gina?"

Gina's eyes were still fixed on the gate. "Hmm?"

"What's going on?"

"Huh?" The little pink tongue poked anxiously out, but the jet eyes didn't even swivel in her direction.

Shani touched the teenager lightly on the arm. "I asked you what was…hey, Andrew! No hanging upside down from the monkey bars, okay?" Andrew, a hyperactive four-year-old with dimples the size of nickels, looked at her as if she was talking Greek. Shani motioned for him to right himself, which he reluctantly did.

She returned her attention to Gina. "You look weird," she said without preamble.

Gina looked down at herself. "Really? It's this shirt, isn't it? Aw, man! I knew I shouldn't have put it on!"

"That's not what I meant. I meant you're *acting* weird. Like you're up to something."

Gina gave her a wide-eyed look. "Up to something? Me?" Then the dark eyes skated toward the gate, and Shani had her answer.

A sleek, dusty pink macho-mobile had pulled up to the curb, and the door was shoved outward. Out stepped Elliot, large as life and twice as gorgeous. Just the sight of him made Shani's breath catch. His hair had gotten a little longer, almost back in the messy style he'd worn it in when she'd first met him. He was holding a shopping bag half his height, like Santa Claus coming way too early.

She felt the breath in her throat trip itself up. He looked good...better than good. There was that thing he did when he walked into a place, the way he stood there and surveyed it before entering. Like a lion checking out the veld, making sure there were no interlopers, and that all the females within range were focused on him. A half smile around his mouth told her he was glad to be here, and confident he'd be welcome. The problem was she didn't recall inviting him.

"Gina!" Shani yelped. "You didn't!"

She could have patented the look of innocence Gina gave her. "I think it's time to pass 'round the jelly beans." she said.

"We didn't buy jelly beans."

"Then I'll pass 'round something else." She darted off with a self-satisfied grin.

Elliot. Here. After an absence of two months. And he looked so fine he made her eyes hurt. Shani didn't know whether to fire Gina or give her a bonus. She wiped her hands on her skirt and walked over, as casually as she could, which was saying something, considering that her blood was pumping so fast she could hear it flow.

"Elliot," she managed.

He smiled at the sight of her, eyes running over her face as if to remind himself what she looked like, or to reassure himself that his memory of her was accurate. "You've got a dolphin on your cheek," he observed.

Her hand rose to touch the greasepaint there. It came away tinged with silver glitter. "I've got stars on the other one." A pretty pointless conversation to be having, she thought, given that just being within three feet of him was making her heart do dangerous things. Like try to break free of her rib cage.

"Suits you." He was still examining her, smiling.

"I didn't invite you, you know."

"Message I got was that the birthday girl was dying to see me."

"Maybe she was," she conceded. Understatement of the decade. Shani would have thought a child that age would forget easily and move on to worship someone else, but Bee had been steadfast in her adoration—and in pining for her adored. She still asked for Elliot almost every day, with a persistence that greatly tried Shani's patience.

"Was her mom? Dying to see me?"

Shani chewed on her lip. Did she miss him? What kind of question was that? If lying in bed unable to sleep most nights, kicking off sheets that were heated even on a chilly night, counted as missing him. Or finding herself staring into space in the middle of a lecture, causing her students to gape back at her and wonder if the new professor was a little bit loony. If the raging, unsatisfied desire that had taken up residence deep in her center like an uninvited wildcat that couldn't be dislodged counted as missing him, well, yeah. She guessed she did.

But if not having him around spared her the look of rejection in his eyes, the hurt that she saw in them and the knowledge that she'd put it there through her own thoughtlessness, well, then...

He tilted his head to one side, coming so close she thought he was going to kiss her. Her lips parted, filling up with blood in anticipation, even though her mind told her to pull away, not to allow him to draw her into himself again. But instead, he only examined her eyes, his own like discerning lasers. Piercing her thoughts. Analyzing them. Above the screeching sound of cartoons playing out on the wide-screen TV and the dinging of pinball machines, his whisper was as clear as a shout. "Shani? Did you miss me?"

She worked on her lower lip, scraping off the lipstick with her teeth. To answer him honestly would be to lose everything she'd gained in the past month and a half, every inch of ground upon which she'd built her sense of self-sufficiency. Telling him the truth would make her weak again. She could lie, she guessed, but she was ensnared in his power. Unable even to think of a lie fast enough.

Instinctively avoiding the trap of his gaze, she looked away, just in time to see Bee dangling from the monkey bars just as Anthony had done. She was about to yell out a warning when Bee spotted Elliot, wriggled down with the kind of haste that would make any mother's blood go cold, dropped easily to the grass and darted toward them.

"Elliottttt!" she squealed.

"There'd better be a unicorn in there," Shani murmured, pointing at his Santa sack. "You promised."

Elliot grinned. "Got it covered." He reached into the

bag at his side and withdrew a white plush unicorn the size of a German shepherd. He dropped to one knee, hugging the unicorn with one arm and holding out the other for Bee to cannon into. "Princess!" He kissed her hair as Bee clambered up him, like a mountaineer scaling Mount Rushmore.

"Ell-i-ot! Ell-i-ot! Ell-i-ot!" she chanted. She spotted the unicorn and screamed again.

Shani watched them cling to each other, feeling shunted aside, invisible. The hug went on forever, and then Bee wriggled down to model for him, holding out her empire-waisted, puff-sleeved dress for his viewing. "Look! My new princess dress! I'm wearing it forever and ever."

She wasn't kidding. Shani had mourned the passing of the "I'm-a-bee" phase and embraced the new "I'm-a-princess" one, reasoning that Bee was growing up and showing an interest in new things. She'd bought Bee the new dress a few weeks ago, and the kid had barely taken it off since. It was slightly bedraggled and had jelly stains, but it made Bee happy, and that was enough.

"It's gorgeous, sweetheart," Elliot enthused. "And you know what? I have just the thing to top it off." He dug through his bag of wonders once again and pulled out a diamanté tiara and a pair of gauzy, glittery wings. "Here you go. Magic fairy wings for a fairy princess."

"Are they really magic?"

"I'm betting they are," he answered indulgently.

By now, Bee was in a lather, barely able to stay still long enough for him to strap them on her. She ripped off the little gold crown Shani had bought her for the party and crammed on the tiara in its place. "I don't want that old one anymore," she said airily. "I got Elliot's."

Shani tried not to roll her eyes. Elliot was grinning like

a fool. The meeting of the Elliot-Bee Mutual Admiration Society was beginning to make her weary. "Why don't you go show your friends all the new stuff you got?" she suggested.

Bee thought it was a great idea and left, lugging the monstrous unicorn behind her. "You'll cut the cake with me, Elliot. Right?"

"Right," he assured her.

She trotted off, saying something about not wanting to cut her pretty cake with any stinky boys. They watched her try to cram the unicorn into one of the tunnels on the play park Shani had set up, and then faced each other again. They were as alone as they could be in a crowded garden.

His eyes were on her. She wasn't sure she liked that. "You didn't answer my question," he reminded her.

"I forget what it was."

"Hmm." He was smiling with the confidence of a man who knew damn well she'd done no such thing. That partly irritated her, and partly made her tingle with the knowledge that he understood her so well. "Walk with me," he suggested softly.

"Are you crazy? There's a party going on!"

"There're a dozen parents here to supervise the kids, and Gina looks like she's got the food under control. There's soda everywhere, pizza everywhere, and the kids are happy. What could go wrong?"

She looked around. He was right, but that didn't make her feel any better. The crowd was her protection. If she was alone with him again, who knew what would happen?

He took her hand, the first time he'd touched her since that awful day in Martinique, and she almost moaned at the contact. "Come," he cajoled. "There's something I need to tell you."

The serpent in the tree tempted…tempted…but that way led to danger. If she gave in to him now, she'd be skating down a slippery slope, falling into him again. But the prospect was too sweet to be denied, even though she knew the pain it could bring with it. The serpent hissed in her ear again, seductively, irresistibly, and Eve fell.

"I'll…go tell Gina."

"Ten minutes," he promised. "Five."

He followed her, picking his way through the throng of screaming, sugar-crazed kids. Gina was at the table, doling out cheese puffs. She looked up over Shani's shoulder at Elliot and grinned in triumph. He grinned back. *Great*, Shani thought. *My nearest and dearest are conspiring against me.* "Gina," she began. "Elliot and I…I mean… we just thought we could…you know, nip out for a few minutes…."

"Take your time," Gina said immediately. Her smile nearly split her face.

"We'll just go around the block, once," Shani said hastily, embarrassment making her collar itchy. And, just to dispel any images Gina might have of them making out down the street in broad daylight, she added, "Just to talk."

"What-*ever!*" Gina sang, and turned her back on them.

Elliot smiled, not a mocking, triumphant smile, but one so filled with tender gratitude it made Shani almost afraid for her power to resist him. "Thank you."

She nodded. She felt his hand at her waist, warm and reassuring, guiding her through the throng toward the gate. She turned her head, her motherly instinct making her check on her child one last time before she was out of sight…in time to see Bee on the monkey bars. The girl was standing on the top bars, placing one foot before the next like a tightrope walker, until she came to a stop in the middle. Before Shani could think, react, cry out, the little girl spread out her arms, and with a serene, confident smile on her face, fairy princess wings quivering—she leaped.

Shani knew the thud she heard existed solely in her head, but it was a terrifying sound all the same. She screamed and ran forward, reaching for her child, trying to gather her into her arms. Elliot pried Bee free. "Don't touch her, Shani. Not yet."

Bee was wailing, blood streaming from her forehead and coursing down her neck, staining the pink dress, speckling the gossamer wings. Holding her arm out for her mother.

"My baby!" Shani reached for her again.

Elliot was firm, his hand closing around her wrist. He was sober, rigid and focused. "I know you want to hold her," he said gently, but leaving no room for argument. "But we need to check her out. Broken bones…" He hesitated. "Spinal injury."

"What?"

He pressed his lips on her forehead. "Easy," he soothed. "She'll be all right."

Shani watched, paralyzed with horror, as Elliot worked his fingers along Bee's body, touching her with infinite gentleness, taking off her shoes and running his car keys lightly along the soles of her feet. Touching her head, feeling along her neck. "Get a towel, Gina," he barked. "And fill it with ice." Gina was back with it in seconds. He folded it and pressed it against the wound on Bee's forehead.

Fear made Shani's stomach roll. "What's going on? Can you tell how bad it is?"

"I think she broke her forearm. It's swelling, see? And we'll need to take care of that gash on her head. It'll take a stitch or two."

How could he be so calm at a time like this? She watched as he gathered Bee up in his arms, shushing her, cooing at her as she protested and flailed. "Doesn't seem to be any damage to her spine," he said comfortingly, and then repeated, "She'll be okay."

"She's not okay!" Shani argued.

"She will be," he promised. "Come."

Chapter 20

"You gave her those wings, Elliot."

"I'm sorry."

Shani was sitting in the back of Elliot's car, next to the car seat he had neglected to remove since last Bee had been in it. She stroked Bee's hair, trying to hold the ice pack steady against the wound on her forehead. Bee's shrieks of fear and pain had subsided into piteous mews that tore at her heart.

Shani lifted her eyes to catch the reflection of Elliot's in the rearview mirror. "You told her they were magic," she accused.

He shook his head regretfully. "I'm so sorry, baby. I really am. I had no idea—"

"That she'd actually try to *fly?*"

"Yes."

To be honest, that possibility had never entered her mind

either, but in her anxiety she was happy to let him suffer. She sniffed and looked away.

What he said next drew her eyes to his again. "I'm sorry, Shani, but I haven't quite got the hang of this parenting thing. You're going to have to teach me."

Did he say…? Had she really heard…? Her mouth hung open like a trapdoor.

Having let that bombshell fall, he focused on the road, bringing the car easily into the parking lot of Immaculate Heart Pediatric. As she got out, her mind was a kaleidoscope of conflicting emotions. Her heart struggled to keep up with the demands her body was placing on it. She watched through a fog as Elliot gently reached in and picked Bee up. His shirt bore dark red smears of her daughter's blood.

The sight was like a splash of cold water. Shani collected herself, slammed the door shut and ran around to Elliot's side. As they hurried toward the doors labeled EMERGENCY she had the weird sensation that she and Elliot had been caught on a merry-go-round and they had come full circle to where they had started. The question was: Where would they go next?

The blood growing sticky on the pale little face was enough to mobilize the hospital workers into action. Documents were thrust into Shani's fist, and Bee was strapped onto a gurney even before she was rushed through the inner doors.

A dragon in a nurse's uniform—maybe the same one from last time, maybe not—stepped forward, but Elliot didn't give her the chance to speak. "I'm her dad," he said crisply, and didn't stop.

Bee was examined, prodded and poked. X-rayed, sedated and stitched up. Her arm was put in a hot pink cast. And all through it, Elliot held Shani's hand. During the particularly gruesome parts, when all that blood was wiped away and the wound revealed, when the IV needle put in an appearance, he squeezed it, and that was enough to keep her nerves steady. Enough to keep her at her daughter's side when she needed her.

A flash of her new credit card had found Bee a place in a private room on one of the upper floors. Eventually, when the latest rounds were made, Bee's vitals checked for the nth time and the attending nurse shut the door behind her, Shani and Elliot were alone next to the small, sleeping shape on the bed.

Elliot reached out and touched the chubby cheek, gold glitter coming away on his fingers. "She looks so tiny," he commented.

"They always do when they're sick," Shani murmured. "Don't ask me why." She touched Bee, too. They'd had to cut off her pretty princess dress, and now she was wearing a hospital gown decorated with ducks. She wondered what Bee would say when she woke to find her precious dress gone.

Elliot knew what she was thinking. "We'll get her a new one. Something even nicer." His hand left Bee's cheek, and he trailed the backs of his fingers against Shani's wrist.

She snatched her hand away. "What's up with this 'we' thing, Elliot? What's with you and all this talk about parenting lessons?"

"You don't know?"

"No!"

"Really?"

She sucked her teeth and backed away, turning to the window. It was getting dark. Fleetingly, she hoped that Gina had managed to pack up the party things okay. She was guessing the party hadn't gone on much longer after the birthday girl was whisked off to hospital.

She sensed Elliot's presence behind her. She saw his

reflection in the window. "What I know," she began, and stopped. "What I know is you left me alone on a beach in Martinique." Technically, *she'd* been the one to walk away, but no matter. She went on. "I made some stupid mistakes. I'm not denying that. Those photos…they were dumb…."

"Those photos don't mean anything," he interrupted. "They're over and done with. It wasn't your fault."

Her eyes were filled with puzzlement and doubt. "I thought…"

"They're nothing. I don't care who's seen them. Because all they have is the memory of an image. I have the real thing."

The force of emotion with which he said it almost took the wind out of her sails, but she came at him again. "As for my ex-husband, he may be a creep to you, but there was a time when he was everything to me."

He flinched.

"But that time's over." She wet her lips. "And if I…let my guard down when he came to see his daughter…"

"Leave it, Shani. It's okay."

"Is it? You can't even hear his name without going green!"

He struggled to explain. "It's just that I looked at him and wondered…" He couldn't finish.

"Wondered what?"

"If you could love someone like that…" He gave a small, slightly embarrassed laugh. "…Then what did it say about me?"

The question floored her. "You're comparing yourself to him? And coming up wanting?"

He looked down at the floor, kicking the skirting board. "When you turned to him, after the fight—"

She'd kicked herself for that thoughtless, instinctive reaction a hundred times. Again, she tried to explain. "I was afraid for *you*. I didn't want you to get into trouble for doing him serious harm. I'm sorry if you thought…"

He cut her off. "You didn't do anything wrong. I wasn't even seeing you. I was seeing my mother, walking away from me. I felt like a kid again. And I was so mad and hurt I couldn't even explain that to you. I could hardly figure it out myself. I've spent so much time locking horns with my dad, I never really worked through how mad I was at *her*…."

Shani wished she could touch him, but she didn't know if her touch would be welcome. "It's perfectly normal. She hurt you, too…."

"The point is—" he rubbed his head "—I realized what a mess I was, and I needed time to get my act together. And I realized I couldn't be with you, free and clear, if I didn't put all that to rest."

She frowned. "What do you mean?"

"Why do you think I've stayed away for so long?"

She swallowed. "Because I hurt you."

He put his arms around her and groaned in anguish. "Oh, sweetheart, no! If I'd thought for a second… I didn't want to see you again because I needed time to get rid of all these demons. I needed time to work things through with my dad. Stop letting my mother's tragedy stand in the way."

She searched his face; he was sober and sincere. "Did you?"

He thought hard before he answered. "We made a start."

"I'm glad."

She felt his strong, hard arms around her and felt herself being pulled against his chest. The scent of him was so familiar, it was almost as if she'd been carrying it around within her all the time they'd been apart. A haunting.

He stroked away a lock of her hair, then released her from his embrace and took her by the hand. "Come with me."

She gave Bee a panicked glance. "Where? I can't leave…."

"Just as far as the chair, sweetheart. You look like you need to sit down…."

"I need no such—" She felt herself being lifted onto his lap as he sat in the large, comfortable armchair. Its fine upholstery and spaciousness was a far cry from the lumpy plastic one on which she'd slept for three nights on the ward the last time they were here.

"I'm not going to rush you," he began.

"You'd better—"

His kiss cut off whatever irascible comment she was about to make. And a sweet kiss it was: a reservoir of weeks of longing and want. She was locked in the circle of his arms again, and she discovered there a place she never wanted to leave. When he finally lifted his mouth, she was vibrating like a plucked violin string.

"I'm not going to rush you," he promised. "But I'm staking my claim nonetheless." He took a deep breath. "So, I'm putting you on notice."

"That…?"

"That I'm going to pursue you with everything I have. I know I haven't always been what you wanted—"

She cut him off, horrified. "You…you've been… wonderful." She cupped his jaw, feeling the prickle of stubble. "Everything I've ever wanted, and more than I've ever needed. You're my angel…"

He let out a surprised laugh. "Angel?"

She nodded. "That night we brought Bee here. The first time. I had an image of you—an angel swooping down to save me when I needed help. To stop me from hurting. You've never been anything but good to me and Bee—"

"I love you both so much—"

"You taught me how to believe again. You showed me heaven…"

He laughed. The small fire that she'd seen within him grew to a blaze, giving him an unearthly glow, an almost tangible heat. "I'll take you there again, whenever you like," he promised. "We can go together."

Shani squirmed in his lap, making herself more comfortable, and wrapped her arms around his neck, linking her hands around her wrists. Joy flowed through her, warm and sweet. "I love you," she sighed against the hollow of his throat.

His fingers were in her hair, strong, soothing, easing away all sadness, anxiety and pain with every stroke. His heartbeat thudded against her breast. "That's all we need." He eased her head down into the crook of his shoulder with infinite gentleness.

"Sleep," he told her softly. "I'll be here when you wake up."

* * * * *

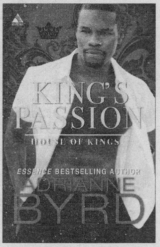

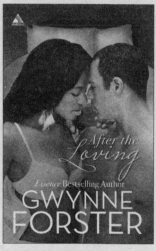

REQUEST YOUR FREE BOOKS!

2 FREE NOVELS
PLUS 2 FREE GIFTS!

KIMANI™
ROMANCE

Love's ultimate destination!

YES! Please send me 2 FREE Kimani™ Romance novels and my 2 FREE gifts (gifts are worth about $10). After receiving them, if I don't wish to receive any more books, I can return the shipping statement marked "cancel." If I don't cancel, I will receive 4 brand-new novels every month and be billed just $4.69 per book in the U.S. or $5.24 per book in Canada. That's a saving of at least 16% off the cover price. It's quite a bargain! Shipping and handling is just 50¢ per book in the U.S. and 75¢ per book in Canada.* I understand that accepting the 2 free books and gifts places me under no obligation to buy anything. I can always return a shipment and cancel at any time. Even if I never buy another book, the two free books and gifts are mine to keep forever.

168/368 XDN FDAT

Name _____ (PLEASE PRINT) _____

Address _____ Apt. # _____

City _____ State/Prov. _____ Zip/Postal Code _____

Signature (if under 18, a parent or guardian must sign)

Mail to the **Reader Service:**
IN U.S.A.: P.O. Box 1867, Buffalo, NY 14240-1867
IN CANADA: P.O. Box 609, Fort Erie, Ontario L2A 5X3

Not valid for current subscribers to Kimani Romance books.

Want to try two free books from another line?
Call 1-800-873-8635 or visit www.ReaderService.com.

* Terms and prices subject to change without notice. Prices do not include applicable taxes. Sales tax applicable in N.Y. Canadian residents will be charged applicable taxes. Offer not valid in Quebec. This offer is limited to one order per household. All orders subject to credit approval. Credit or debit balances in a customer's account(s) may be offset by any other outstanding balance owed by or to the customer. Please allow 4 to 6 weeks for delivery. Offer available while quantities last.

Your Privacy—The Reader Service is committed to protecting your privacy. Our Privacy Policy is available online at www.ReaderService.com or upon request from the Reader Service.

We make a portion of our mailing list available to reputable third parties that offer products we believe may interest you. If you prefer that we not exchange your name with third parties, or if you wish to clarify or modify your communication preferences, please visit us at www.ReaderService.com/consumerschoice or write to us at Reader Service Preference Service, P.O. Box 9062, Buffalo, NY 14269. Include your complete name and address.

KROM11

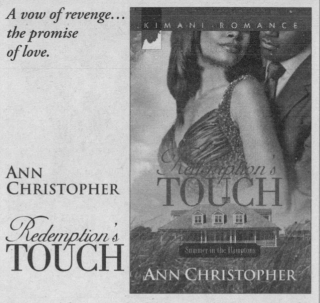

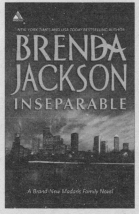